SILLY LITTLE
RICH GIRL

jimmy **gleacher**

CASPERIAN
BOOKS

Thank you Clay Stuart, Reed Johnson, and Scotty Zenko. See you *Ad Astra*. With the three of you already there, it's probably like afterhours at The Rouge.

www.casperianbooks.com

Cover image by Pam Uhlenkamp.

ISBN-10: 1-934081-17-5
ISBN-13: 978-1-934081-17-4

This book is dedicated to Gary Dell'Abate's teeth

Home

—∿∿—

Silly Little Rich Girls—that's what the caption says above the picture of Lily Durfee and me on the front page of today's New York Post. If you're alive and live in the Tri-State area, maybe you're looking at us now. Hopefully you turned on the news this morning and heard about what happened several hours after that photo was taken. By then the papers were already printed, stacked and bundled, and being dropped off the backs of trucks all over the city. The presses had run and could not be halted, and while Lily was bound and gagged and stuffed into an SUV, and I was being shot trying to save her, the plastic cording holding the piles of newspapers together was scarring a groove into our smiling faces.

I'm hoping you still have a sense of humor, wherever you are, dead or alive, and are laughing at the headline. You know I'm no silly little rich girl. I may be more famous for my slip-ups than my successes, but all that is changing. I design handbags now and they're selling quite well. I also had a big role on a TV show. I'm not rich yet, but the money is coming in and I'm only twenty-four years old, so who's the silly one now?

We are sisters, Jamie. We have cried the same tears and forced smiles in the same family photographs. We've sat in silence at the same dinner table, afraid to speak and afraid to hear what might be said next. And we were raised by the same mother who thought that paying the bills was the same as paying attention. Mom is a different person now; we've all changed since you left. Our little brother Jack is six feet tall and goes to Brown. Jack's an incredible sculptor and, believe it or not, Mom encourages his art.

I shouldn't even be talking to you right now. If my shrink knew, she'd kill me. I take meds just to keep from thinking about you, but the pills aren't doing their job. Maybe it's the adrenaline from getting shot, or maybe I'm just really lonely here in this hospital room, or maybe it's just time to face you. It's about seven in the morning here in Manhattan and my surgery isn't until late this afternoon, so we've got all day, which is good, because a lot has happened since the night you vanished.

Let's start from when you left five years ago. It was summertime and you had just graduated from Dartmouth and I had just finished my sophomore year there. We lived together off campus in an apartment above Professor Carr's garage. Remember all the dumb jokes he made because his last name was Carr and he rented out his garage? Then there was the night he got drunk and mowed his lawn beneath the full moon; it wasn't really bright enough to see, and he couldn't walk a straight line anyway, and in the morning half his garden had been shaved. It was a fun year and we had never enjoyed such freedom. Mom was distracted from trying to run our lives because she had just been named CEO of B-Global, the telecom whose stock caught lightning in a bottle and became *the* stock to buy and sell. You couldn't turn on CNBC without seeing its ticker symbol scroll across the bottom of the screen sandwiched between Sirius and Google. We had a freedom we were unaccustomed to, but when school was over and we were back under her roof without the cushion of all those miles between New Hampshire and New York, things changed back to normal. Mom found a flaw with everything you did—your Birkenstocks were "Jesus Sandals," your clothes were "hippy-dippy," she'd get on your case if your hair was messy, and make you change before dinner even when we were eating at home.

I don't know why Mom rode you so much harder than me and Jack, maybe because you were her first and she was insulted you didn't want to be just like her. She was the Armani-wearing ass-kicking boardroom ball breaker and you were the hemp-wearing flower child with the peace symbol tattooed on the bottom of your foot. Remember the fight that caused? Mom was so mad she banned you from the beach club because she didn't want her friends to see your body art. You split that summer and didn't get in touch with us for months, but everyone knew you were fine because you were crashing on Laura's couch on Riverside Drive and were spotted all over the city.

But getting back to the night you left for good, the summer was off to a craptacular start, and as usual, Mom would get home from work late and instantly crawl up everyone's ass. Jack was in trouble for skipping out on Little League to watch the mimes on the steps of the Met, I was in the shithouse because I enrolled myself for classes at the Manhattanville School of Design, and Mom's marriage to Andrew was such a sham—he was "traveling for work" when we all knew he was really living in a hotel in Midtown. You dropped the biggest bomb of all when you told Mom you'd been accepted into the Peace Corps and were leaving for the Ivory Coast to farm in a village somewhere near the city of Abidjan. She said all that money she'd spent on tuition would be wasted in Africa. You were proud of what you were doing and wanted her approval. When Mom shat all over your aspirations, you pretended to shrug it off and said you'd predicted she'd be such a wench, but you couldn't hide the tears in your eyes and the next day you were gone.

We all had different theories of where you went, but none of us thought you were gone for good. For the first couple of weeks I wasn't even that worried. You had run off before and were legendarily stubborn and everyone chalked your absence up to just another epic battle between you and Mom. I went on as though everything was normal, going to my design classes at night and working all day at Morgan Worth Bank for Mom's friend Tim Purdy, the young hotshot who ran the Risk Arbitrage desk. He was charming, good-looking, rich, powerful, and married of course, but he was a flirt and I was the green summer intern. The sexual tension between us put butterflies in my stomach, so I was well distracted.

After twenty days without a word from you, a bell went off in my head right in the middle of the night and woke me so quickly I thought the apartment was on fire. I ran to your room and turned on your lights and rifled through your desk and closet so wildly, the noise woke Mom and brought her to your room. She was wearing a light blue silk nightgown that hung from her shoulders to the floor. She looked beautiful. Slumber softened her; she hadn't been awake long enough for her hard edges to show, and her face could have been yours. But then she spoke. "Jesus Christ, Liza, what's gotten into you? It's three in the morning."

I was holding your global warming snow globe of New York City that showed the streets flooding rather than snow falling. "I can't find Jamie's passport. I think maybe she went to Africa early. That's why she hasn't called or emailed us yet, because she can't. There's probably no service where she's at." I held my arms out and said, "No wonder!"

"Jamie's not in Africa, Liza. You can't just show up to the Peace Corps early and hang out. It's a whole thing. Trust me. This is all a big game to her; if you worry you're letting her win."

I shook the globe with both hands and said, "You need to find Jamie and apologize; tell her you're proud of her."

"If she wants to go off and save the world she should at least work in it first so she knows what she's rescuing."

"You should be more supportive. Seriously, I'd rather go to a community college and pay my own way if it meant you'd encourage me."

Mom was always up for a fight and replied, "You're welcome to strike out on your own anytime, Liza."

"You mean like Andrew?"

Mom didn't blink. "Andrew's in London working on a deal."

I checked the glass ball's progress; half of the Empire State Building was under water. "Are people really gonna care that much if the CEO gets divorced? I mean, it's pretty shitty to lie to your kids, especially when they're not as dumb as you think they are."

"Wait a minute, let me cue the violins." She held her hand mockingly to her ear.

"So are you paying Andrew to keep quiet? Because that makes him a gigolo, right? Not that he wasn't one already, I mean, everyone knew you guys were doing it behind Dad's back and that he's a gold digger."

The edges had returned to Mom's face and I could see none of you in her. "Keep talking and you'll regret it," she said.

"I know you want us to be little carbon copies of you, but just so you know, I'm not working in finance when I graduate, either. I'm going into fashion design." I checked the globe; the entire city was sunk.

Mom got really sarcastic. "That's very cute, Liza. I'll pay for your crayons and construction paper."

And it was that comment that made me realize just how badly you wanted to hurt her, so rather than risk finding you and thus ruining the power your leaving gave you, I stopped looking, and soon enough began to believe you were snacking on plantains beneath a Kapok tree, shaded from the Ivory Coast sun. As the days and months passed my imagination grew and grew and, eventually, I began sending myself letters from you with elaborate stories about crops you planted and tribesmen who taught you how to make the skies cry by dancing. I copied your handwriting and

8

used your fountain pen and your letters never ceased to please me, but I didn't once tell Mom or Jack.

We were all living a lie. Jack had a steady girlfriend. Mom rented Andrew a loft on 10th Street and he attended dinner parties and work functions clutching her hand. Dad called from Minnesota with stories about cross-country skiing all winter, but he was really just drunk in his hut, staring through a hole in a thick slab of ice. And me, well I lived in the sorority house and buried myself in schoolwork and electives. I had a 4.0 for junior and senior year and founded the Dartmouth Sewing with Design Club, which grew to thirty-seven members (four were guys) who created amazing dresses, handbags, belts, and even flip-flops. When friends asked about you, I told them you were learning so much and completely moved by the people of Africa. Sometimes I'd leave your letters out for people to read, but never the envelopes because the postmarks were all wrong.

But the act is over now, Jamie. Jack's new love interest is named Tom. Mom unloaded Andrew the day she was forced to resign, and Dad doesn't even phone us anymore. I can't call him after six if I want him to remember our conversation. Last year I tried to visit him and called to say I was flying to St. Paul the next day. We set a time and place for him to pick me up at the airport, but he was nowhere in sight when I landed. I gave him an hour before calling his house and he answered like it was any other day.

"Dad, where are you?" I said.

"In my living room," he answered. A talk radio program was turned up too loud in the background. Dad was drunk and chipper and said, "So, what's news, kiddo?"

We talked for a bit as I waited in line to buy a ticket home. There was a woman ahead of me tugging a huge metal case that looked heavy. The trunk was dented and scratched and covered in decals from all over the world, but right in the middle of them was a sticker that said, "Home is where the heart is." I wondered if that meant people who run from home are running from their hearts. I think the opposite is true and that people who run away are chasing what's in their hearts, and all I can say to you now is I hope your pursuit will bring you to where your heart is.

The Letters

———

By the time I graduated I had a pen pal in Abidjan I'd met over the Internet sending me envelopes I had sent to her, letters from you to me, so the stamps and the country codes would be authentic. I had her send the final note to Mom's apartment, because that's where I was living, and on the day it arrived, Mom happened to see the mail before me. I was working for Mr. Purdy again, my third summer in a row, but this time I was brought on full-time as a bona fide employee. We were covering a merger in which a big soft drink company was taking over a small, all-natural soft drink company and working late. Mr. Purdy's marriage was in trouble and we often worked late. He was developing quite a reputation and the women in the office called him Mr. Pervy. When I got home, Mom was sitting in the den with the envelope, unopened, resting on her lap. She was pale, held up your letter, and said, "Something came in the mail for you."

I sat on the couch next to her chair, took the envelope, and tried to act natural. "Oh, another letter from Jamie. Cool."

"She's been writing you?" She sounded hollow.

"Yeah," I said. "You know, like once a month or so. She's pretty busy over there."

"Liza, I hired a private detective to track her down a year and a half ago. According to him she never showed up at the Peace Corps orientation." Mom eyed the letter in my hand. "She hasn't made a single phone call or taken out one dollar from her bank account since the night she left." Mom paused and looked me in the eyes; she wanted to make sure I was listening. My ears heard every word, but my eyes stared at the letter and my mind chose to believe that the words I'd written on a piece of paper were

10

more real than the words coming from Mom's mouth. She continued, "The detective couldn't prove she was dead though, so I went to see a psychic in Tulsa, Oklahoma. Apparently she's the best, and she instructed me to bring a pair of Jamie's shoes, a sample of her handwriting, and her favorite fruit."

"Banana," I said.

"I know."

"Sorry."

Mom patted my knee. Her movements were slow and careful and she was obviously very spooked by something. "This woman—I was expecting someone old with long gray hair wearing colorful sashes and robes, but instead she was young and looked like she shopped at The Gap. Her house was clean and had a lot natural sunlight. She laid the shoes, the postcard Jamie sent me the summer she lived in Berkeley, and a banana I had bought at a gas station on the way to her house on a table in front of her, and in less than five seconds she looked at me and said, 'You have to let her go.'"

"What does that mean?" I asked.

"I took it to mean she was dead."

"Maybe she was just saying you should let Jamie be Jamie, you should let her go do the things she wants."

Mom's mind was in Tulsa and she said, "That piece of fruit is the only thing I've ever purchased in the entire state of Oklahoma, and I remember when I was buying it, I thought to myself, 'Well, at least when I die I can say I once bought a banana in Oklahoma.'" Mom quickly glanced at the envelope. The letter was well traveled and the stamps were exotic and she almost seemed afraid to stare at it too long. Then she took it from me, and as she read the letter, her face only got paler. She seemed sad for someone who had just discovered the daughter she thought was dead was still alive. When she reached the end, she frowned and said, "Jamie didn't write this. You did. I know my daughters. I may work a lot and be demanding, and maybe I didn't bake you cookies and take you shopping, but I know my daughters."

She sent me to a shrink the next day. His name was Dr. Graves, a gaunt man with round reading glasses and a handlebar mustache. His teeth were yellow and he was wearing a wool blazer in the middle of summer. I tried to confuse him by admitting all kinds of crazy things. I told him Dad would

11

be better off dead, and when I closed my eyes sometimes, all I could see was Jack getting run over by a bus. I told him I had a fear of paperclips and the word hotdog made my foot ache. I told him I heard voices in my head.

"What are they saying?" he asked.

"Some days they tell me to jump in front of a bus. Some days they tell me to eat a hotdog."

"When did this start?"

"My eighteenth birthday. They woke me up singing a nursery rhyme. 'I don't want to go to Mexico no more, more, more. There's a big fat policeman at my door, door, door. He grabbed me by the collar, he made me pay a dollar, I don't want to go to Mexico no more, more, more.'"

Dr. Graves leaned forward and rested his elbows on his knees. "Can you make the voices stop?"

"Sure. All I have to do is draw and they go right away. Like a sketch for a dress or a handbag or maybe a piece of jewelry. That kind of thing. I want to be a designer. I started a club at Dartmouth." I shrugged like it was nothing.

The doctor sat back and was trying hard not to show any reaction. "You're a very bright girl."

"Thank you," I said. "I'm not making this up, if that's what you're thinking."

He opened his mouth, but at the last second held back what he was about to say and thought another moment. Then he said, "People who hear voices can't control them. Sometimes they're able to ignore them but they can't make them stop."

"You're not sure though, are you?"

"No, I know the pathology quite well."

"Not sure about me," I said. "About whether I'm lying or not."

"You're a fascinating young woman, has anyone ever told you that?"

"My boss, about twelve times a day, but he wants to fuck me. Is that what you want, for me to come down with a little case of transference? Maybe that's where all this sweet talk is coming from."

"Sweet talk?"

"It would never work. You're too old for me. You're cute though." He wasn't but I didn't want to be mean.

"Tell me about the letters."

"Maybe I wanted Mom to see that letter. Maybe she's spent the past two years pretending like nothing's wrong when it turns out she's hiring private dicks and flying across the country to bring a psychic with no style a banana. Maybe I'm the only one who thinks Jamie isn't dead and that's exactly what's keeping her alive."

"Are you afraid she'll die if you allow yourself to believe she's dead?"

"What's the difference?"

"Well, culpability for starters."

I stood up and shook his hand. "It's been a pleasure, Doc, but I have to go."

When I got home, I decided to throw out every item I owned before you vanished. I started with the things you gave me: the sweater with the snowflake on the chest that you bought in Vermont, the turquoise necklace you brought home from New Mexico, the Douglas Coupland book about Miss Wyoming. My closet had never looked so big. I worked myself into a frenzy. Mom and Jack had to lock me out of their rooms. They saw me filling up garbage bag after garbage bag and they could tell by the look in my eyes nothing was safe. Your ghost lived on in yearbooks, favorite T-shirts, and coffee mugs made in kindergarten. I had just graduated from college and wanted to start fresh, anyway.

At some point in the middle of the night I fell asleep. Jack came in my room early the next morning and silently took everything out of the bags and put it back in its original place. Jack was always doing things like that.

I was late for work the next day and Mr. Pervy could tell something was wrong. He called me into his office, and the second he shut his door, I broke into tears and downloaded everything about you, Mom, Andrew, the psychic. He suggested I call the *New York Times* or the *Wall Street Journal* to spread the word you'd been missing, and that Mom was so concerned, she was consulting with psychics. He said the more people looked for you the better, and then sent me out of his office.

So I called CNBC and they were intrigued. A reporter and a cameraman met me at noon in the lobby of Mom's office building. The reporter was young and I recognized her from the Dartmouth vs. Williams field hockey games because she had been the captain of the Williams team.

Mom wouldn't come downstairs. She sent the VP of PR, a slick thirty-seven-year-old woman with perfect blond highlights, knee-high black leather boots, a short black skirt, and a thin pale line around her tan ring finger. She pulled me aside and whispered with an impressive ferocity, "Your mother is about to explode and the shit is falling into my lap, so just stand behind me and let me handle this." She was beautiful and intimidating and at least six inches taller than me in her boots. She probably got her way with everything and that included me, because I stood at her back like a mute as she explained on camera that you had been presumed dead for the past eighteen months. She stressed this was a family matter and asked for privacy and said everything was business as usual at B-Global and the third quarter was off to a robust start.

The camera panned my way and the field hockey player said, "Tell us why you think your sister is alive."

I froze because now there were shoulder-mounted cameras and photogenic women involved, and my heart sank from the gravity of the situation. "I'm sorry. I shouldn't have done this." I looked into the camera and added, "Sorry, Mom," because I knew she was watching from her office upstairs.

When I got back to work, Mr. Pervy treated me coldly. His assistant told me he'd shorted B-Global after convincing me to call the media, because he thought the stock would drop because of the CEO's family crisis, but shares actually went up on the PR woman's assertion that Q3 numbers were robust. When I got home, I searched through the mail hoping to find a real letter from you and I got the next best thing: confirmation you were still alive on the cover of *New York* magazine.

It was actually a picture of Lily Durfee. The magazine was doing a story about that summer's college graduates and what the future held for them. Being her frenemy, I knew the story was coming, everyone did—Lily was never shy about self-promotion. The article was about one student from each borough of New York City, and chose people from different races and economic backgrounds.

There was a Russian girl from Brooklyn who'd studied literature at Bard. She was preparing to move to St. Petersburg, Florida, to teach at a community college. Her summer job was being a receptionist at a dentist's office.

The Bronx was represented by a boy from Kenya who'd graduated from the University of Colorado, where he'd had a full ride on a cross-country scholarship. He was home for the summer saving money and driving his father's yellow cab, looking forward to heading back to Boulder, Colorado, in the fall, where he'd spend the next year training for the Olympics. He was all but guaranteed a spot on the Kenyan marathon squad.

The other male spotlighted was from Staten Island. He'd graduated from Rutgers summa cum laude with a degree in philosophy. A third-generation fireman, he had already started his career with Engine 152.

From Queens was an African American woman with an engineering degree from MIT. In September, she was off to Seattle, Washington, to work for Boeing, which was ironic because she'd never been on a plane.

Lily was Manhattan's delegate, and this is where and when things started to get weird. Lily was on the cover of the magazine wearing a Dartmouth Athletics T-shirt, the kind with the green oval underneath the lettering where people are supposed to write their names. This should be starting to ring a bell. These were the shirts from our sorority party the weekend of the Woman's NCAA Lacrosse Finals. Remember? We all had to write our names on those very ovals and throw them in a barrel. Then, one by one, we each blindly drew a shirt out, and whoever's name we picked was our drinking partner for the next three days. I know you remember because Lily drew your name. What a scandal that was. I still swear it was rigged. You had just started dating the boy who dumped her and then you had to be attached at the hip all weekend long, wearing T-shirts with each other's name on them, which was funny because people were always confusing you two, anyway.

So on the cover of the magazine Lily was wearing a T-shirt with your name written on the front. She was barefoot and wearing jeans, and though I can't be sure, the pants looked like the very pair you were convinced she'd stolen from you. So there she was, filling up the entire page wearing your old jeans and a shirt with your name on it and making a peace sign with her fingers, and I knew it was a signal. I ripped the article out and carried it with me everywhere. I memorized each word and punctuation mark, searched them for patterns, read it backwards, and tried to find clues in the ads filling the margins. I thought the page numbers were your longitude and latitude, but they placed you in the middle of the Atlantic Ocean. Then it all became crystal clear—you were at one of those five destinations: St. Petersburg, Seattle, Boulder, Staten Island, or Manhattan.

So I kept working for Mr. Pervy and lived in Mom's apartment for the next six months saving every penny I could. I stopped going out at night,

15

bought no new clothes, and ate only hot pretzels for meals. In February, I set out for St. Petersburg. Seattle would be next, followed by Boulder, and then Staten Island. And if my quest did not bring me to you, I would hunt down Lily Durfee and hold her prisoner until she brought you to me. What I didn't know was that Lily would find me first.

The Cat in the Cookie Jar

—◦◦◦—

Two cops are standing in the hallway guarding my room in this hospital. One is a cute black guy who looks fresh out of college. This may be his first assignment, and he has that look of excitement and pride like for the first time he's contributing to a world outside his own. The other is a middle-aged Irish man; he's overweight, balding, and smells like cigarettes. He hands the black cop the paper with my picture on the front and points at the middle of his palm snickering, probably making a joke about hand jobs or something equally clever. The black cop stares straight ahead, ignoring the joke, and the fat one laughs at him for not laughing and pats him on the back condescendingly. Then he walks away, probably outside for a smoke, or maybe to call his bookie.

The black officer peers over his shoulder into my room, so I catch his attention and wave him inside. He stops a few feet past the door and asks, "Miss Davis?"

"Liza," I say, but my throat is so dry I hardly make a sound. I swallow some spit and try again, "Liza. My name is Liza."

"Sure thing, Miss Davis," he replies.

"What's your name?" I ask him.

"Marcus." He walks over to the window and lowers the blinds. "Chief just called. Says there's talk of people who might be trying to take your picture through the window?" He says this like a question. "Something about the paparazzi coming in a helicopter? But I think that's just Chief being Chief." He chuckles and looks to me for a corresponding smile.

I give him one even though the idea doesn't seem that absurd. "Where's your partner?" I ask him.

"Officer Ryan?" He steals a glance at the empty doorway. "We're not partners. When he gets back, I'm going out for a soda. Can I bring you anything?"

"I would love a Gatorade."

"Gatorade?" He seems surprised. "I didn't think girls like you drank Gatorade."

"Girls like me?"

"Yeah. Fancy girls."

"Oh, right. Well, I'll need it in a crystal goblet, obviously."

Marcus laughs and begins to leave the room, so I call out his name to stop him. I don't even know what I'm going to say next, but I don't want him to leave, and when he turns around, he still has a smile on his face. "Do they know any more about Lily Durfee?" I ask him.

He shakes his head. "Sure don't, Miss Davis. But I'll let you know."

Lily Durfee. She's the one the helicopters are after. I'm sure you're wondering when I became friends with Lily, your sworn enemy. Please don't hate me for liking her; she's not the same person you knew at Dartmouth. She went and did the Hollywood thing like we all knew she would, but to her credit, she saw through it all and came back East with an ax to grind. She spent two years competing for work and moving up the ranks, but no one could get past the fact she was a pretty girl from a famously rich family. Her diploma from Dartmouth was explained by the buildings on campus named after her grandfather. Jobs she fought hard to win were written off to nepotism and connections. All her achievements were instantly dismissed. People loved to talk about her. She was fodder for comedy show monologues and became a national punch line even though she was smarter than ninety-nine percent of the population.

Lily decided that if everyone was going to assume she was dumb, then she might as well get paid to act dumb, so she pitched and sold a reality TV show titled *Silly Little Rich Girl* in which she flitted around the city mingling with socialites and celebrities. Lily was the executive producer and found all the sponsors herself. The show was actually a very well-camouflaged thirty-minute product placement ad, and the ditzy girl on screen was the mastermind behind the supped-up infomercial that people mistook for a reality show and couldn't stop watching. I was her sidekick and my purses were heavily visible in every episode, which is one reason they continue to sell. Every product featured on the show became a must-have.

Silly Little Rich Girl was a hit, but Lily was over being famous and wanted to burn every bridge that led back to that false promised land, possibly out of fear of being tempted to return, so she made a "behind the scenes" video of *Silly Little Rich Girl* that the public has not yet seen— damning footage that Lily shot herself, with no one's knowledge or outside help. In the span of forty-six days, which was how long it took us to shoot *Silly Little Rich Girl,* she amassed enough material to put actors out of work and socialites in jail. She even has footage of the Mayor of New York City's daughters acting so out of control, it would ruin their father's political aspirations, which are lofty considering the man is a shoo-in to be the next Republican nominee for president. The timing of her kidnapping is no fluke. Just a few days ago, word leaked of Lily's home movies. Anyone could be after her.

Officer Ryan just replaced Marcus at the door and he's sneaking into my room because he thinks I'm sleeping. He removes a disposable camera from his pocket and right before he takes my picture I say, "Cheese!"

He slowly straightens his legs and chuckles. "Looks like you caught the cat in the cookie jar." His accent is a hundred percent New Yawk and he sounds like a mobster even though he's Irish.

"The smell of bacon always wakes me up."

That makes him laugh, and he says, "Do me a favor and turn your head just a cunt hair to the left. You're sittin' in a shadow over there."

"Oh, I get it. You're untouchable."

"That's right, and not in the dot way neither."

"Charming. I'm shocked you even know about the caste system."

He lifts his chin with pride and launches into a story, "So I got this daughter, right? Bright girl, but she loves the celebrities and is always watching that dumb show of yours and saving her money to buy some shit she saw you and that other bim' wearing at a party or whatever. So there I am standing in the doorway over there thinking to myself how I can't believe that the girl in the hospital bed I'm guarding is the same dinghy broad on that show, when your doctor walks in and starts reading off every goddamn prescription known to man, and I say to myself, 'That's funny, I never heard Layla,' that's my daughter—"

"Lovely," I interject. "We should all be named after the song we were conceived to in the bathroom of O'Callaghan's."

He gives the jab a slight nod of approval. "Layla never said nothing

19

about you being a nut job, so I take my break and go on some kid's computer in the coffee shop and get on the Google, and nowhere, not anywhere, do I see mention of you being a total fucking mental case . . . so I'm guessing it's a secret, and a pretty big one, too." He lifts the camera back up to his eye. "Now say 'cheese.'"

Once he's taken the picture and is gone, I call for a nurse because I'm rattled and don't know what else to do. A few minutes later a young guy arrives. His scrubs have been tailored to hug his toned body. He's handsome, has a model's haircut, and his nails are coated with a clear cover of polish. He actually looks very familiar but it could be because he looks like every guy in *Details*. He's alarmed I'm sweating and asks why my heart rate is so fast.

"I had a bad dream," I say. Then I look at him closer and ask, "Have I seen you somewhere before?" He probably thinks I'm hitting on him and it's kinda embarrassing, but I know him from somewhere.

He grins and says, "Well, I did star in a little movie called *Top Gun*."

"No, that's not it."

"Perhaps you're familiar with *Mission Impossible*?"

"Seriously, did you ever live in Boulder, Colorado?"

He looks at me suspiciously. "Maybe . . ."

Then it hits me and, like a contestant on a game show with the winning answer, I shout, "Soy mocha latte and a banana nut muffin! That's what you ordered every Monday, Wednesday, and Friday, usually around eight o'clock in the morning!"

Officer Ryan turns around and peers through the door window. The nurse stares at me, amazed. "You are a freak of nature. I heard you used to work at Vic's coffee shop but I didn't believe it."

I take a victory stretch and tell him, "I was a barista for almost a year."

"I was in nursing school at the university. I can't believe you remember my order." He's beaming like he just received a compliment.

"You're nickname was Boy-Soy. There were more than a few people behind the counter who perked up when you walked in."

He tuts and replies, "That place was a total meat market," and suddenly it's clear why he never hit on the girls behind the counter.

I worked at that coffee shop five days a week, Jamie. I studied every face, deliberated people's gaits, and calculated each customer's slouch. The devil was in the details, and I thought for sure I could pick you out

20

in a lineup an entire city deep. Where were you and what kind of joke is this to have me reunited with Boy-Soy?

When Boy-Soy leaves, I look for Marcus in the doorway because I want his company, but he's still on his break, so I'm forced to be alone with myself. Most days I can handle this, but today is different. Today we are back. There's a green paperclip on the floor in the dusty corner of the room, and in the vents little girls are singing, "I don't want to go to Mexico no more, more, more." My drawing hand is shot, but if I had a pen and paper, I'd sketch with my mouth. I could break into my purse and take a Klonopin or two to knock me out, but I don't want to, because I'd rather be here, with you.

There's a knock at the door and fortunately Marcus is back peering through the window holding a bottle of Gatorade. I smile and he enters the room and places the drink on my bedside table, saying, "Fruit Punch all right?"

"Thank you so much. See any helicopters out there?"

"Sure didn't, Miss Davis," he laughs. "Some news vans, though."

Marcus notices the blinds have been twirled open and shuts them. "Has someone been in here?" He's holding the wand of the blinds looking to me for a reply, so I tell him I've been sleeping but he doesn't believe me.

"How long has Officer Ryan been a policeman?" I ask.

"Since before I was born." Marcus grins and adds, "At least that's what he likes to tell me."

"Wouldn't someone who's been on the force that long have better things to do than guard a minor celebrity?"

"Way I heard it," Marcus says in a confiding voice, "Officer Ryan asked to be on this. Went straight to Chief himself." Marcus casually glances towards the door, then back at me, his eyebrows raised.

"What do you know about me, Marcus?"

"You're on that show, *Silly Little White Girl.*" I start to laugh and he laughs along with me. Then he says, "I know, I know. *Silly Little* Rich *Girl.* You just look so serious." Marcus grabs a chair from the corner of the room, places it a proper distance from the side of my bed, and sits. "They say it's gonna rain today," he offers. "Supposed to thunder something fierce, way I heard it."

"I like the way you talk."

"Officer Ryan tells me my neck is so red it turned black."

21

I crack open the bottle of Gatorade. "Something tells me you don't care much about what Officer Ryan has to say."

He raises his eyebrows and replies, "Something tells me you're right."

I sip the sports drink and tell Marcus to take some money from my purse, but he refuses. Then I ask, "Still no leads on Lily?"

"Not yet, but they'll find her. The whole city's just about turned upside down looking for her. You'd think the president's gone missing the way everyone's carrying on." He hangs his head after saying this and his shoulders slump. "That didn't come out right."

For a while we sit with no words. The room fills with a calm and stillness that probably follows Marcus just about everywhere he goes. It is a calm I am unfamiliar with and could never achieve on my own, and it makes me happy to know that this young black man from the rural South could have something a privileged white girl from Manhattan can't.

Everything is interrupted when Mom knocks on the door and peers through the window. Marcus hops to his feet and holds his hand up like a crossing guard.

"It's okay, Marcus. She's my mom."

Marcus waves Mom in and apologizes to her, and she tells him it's all right and that she's glad someone is keeping me company. Marcus leaves to give us some privacy and Mom sits on the side of my bed, grabs my good hand, and asks, "Are you all right?"

Officer Ryan enters the room and says, "I hate to break your tea party up, girls, but visiting hours aren't until this afternoon."

"I'm her mother," Mom says, probably expecting him to apologize and quietly back out the door.

But Officer Ryan is unmoved and replies, "Congratulations, ma'am, but it doesn't change the time of day."

Mom rises, kisses me on the forehead, and says, "I'll be back at three."

"Bring Jack," I say.

"Don't worry, we already made plans." She kisses me on the forehead again and walks past Officer Ryan like he isn't even there.

He stares at Mom's butt, then turns to me and says, "We'll talk later." He looks at Marcus out in the hall and adds, "Once shine-boy here knocks off for the day," and laughs at the slur, leaving me alone in the room with the lingering smell of Mom's Chanel No. 5.

The Gifting of the LandJet

—⁓—

The scent of Mom's Chanel No. 5 brings me back to her apartment the night my search for you began. It was a Wednesday in the middle of March, and I'd been living at Mom's apartment and working for Mr. Pervy since I'd graduated the previous June. You'd been gone two and a half years, and even though the party line from our family and the PR department at B-Global was that you were dead, I was vocal about you living in St. Petersburg, Boulder, Seattle, Staten Island, or Manhattan, and everyone knew my plans to go look for you, which became a sore spot between me and Mom. She dealt with your leaving by diving into her work and traveling. Jack was away at school and Andrew was still secretly living downtown holding up his end of the arrangement. He ended up getting $2.7 million when they divorced, one-tenth of Mom's golden parachute, but he probably should have shared some of that money with me, since I was the reason she got fired.

When Mom was home between business trips, she'd focus her attention on me. After the CNBC debacle we didn't speak for a month, but eventually she cooled down and her anger was replaced with concern. She didn't understand why I couldn't accept you were dead and tried to send me back to Dr. Graves, but he said he wasn't taking new clients. I told her I wouldn't be kept down; I wasn't Andrew and couldn't be bought. Her private detective hadn't definitively said you were dead, and until someone discovered your remains, I wouldn't give up hope. After six months of doing battle, Mom finally said, "Fine. You're a grownup; you can do whatever you like. But I'm telling you right now, you're setting yourself up for more heartache and your behavior is irrational and troubling." She was packing for a business trip to London and I sat on her couch by the window facing the park and watched her fill her suitcase.

"She's out there, Mom. Someone has to believe."

"Honey, I wish Jamie was alive every day, but she isn't. Maybe now's a good time to face that." Mom moved a sweater from her bed to her bag and a black lacey negligee fell from underneath it to the floor between us.

"Are you taking that with you?"

Mom folded the negligee and placed it in her bag along with the sweater. "Don't change the subject."

"What kind of *business trip* is this?"

Mom zipped her luggage shut and said, "I think you should stop working for Mr. Purdy." I stared at her suitcase wondering about all the secrets it must know. "The job is too stressful and it will do you some good to relax."

"I like my job."

"I know. And you're good at it too, and you can always go back, but right now, I think the most important thing is getting you some help."

"Help? Help for what?"

Mom sat on the edge of the bed across from me and I noticed that we were wearing the same pair of shoes, right down to the color of the leather and the size. "You need to let go of this Jamie fixation."

"Maybe you need to get one."

"Trust me, Liza. I left no stone unturned."

"You didn't even tell anyone you were looking."

"I didn't want a media circus."

"Bad for business, right?"

"How dare you even insinuate such a thing?"

"If you can look for her, then so can I."

"I'm asking you to drop it, Liza. We all need to move on, as a family."

I laughed at her. "Since when do you care about family? You've got one ex-husband drunk in Minnesota and a soon-to-be-ex-husband living off of hush money in a loft downtown."

Mom stood up and grabbed the handle of her baggage. "Here's the last word: when I get back from London there'll be no more talk about Jamie like she's alive or you're going to have to move out."

"Who's the lingerie for, Mom?"

Mom wheeled her bag out of the room and I didn't follow. A few minutes later, the elevator arrived and she and her slinky black negligee were off to London.

The time had come to find you. I had made and saved a lot of money working for Mr. Pervy and I had enough to get by for a while. What I didn't have was a car, but I knew how to get one. Mr. Pervy's wife was a competitive horse rider; in addition to her narrow waist and ski-jump nose, God had given her equestrian talent. She won a lot of shows and traveled a circuit from Palm Beach to Albany, cantering and posting for ribbons. At these competitions she waited around all day just to ride for a few minutes, so for an anniversary present, Mr. Pervy had bought her a special van to use as a refuge during the downtime.

The van was called a LandJet because the cabin was designed like a private jet and came equipped with a couch, television, DVD player, and two swivel chairs with a walnut table that pulled out between them. Mr. Pervy had shown me the brochure when he was buying it. Then, a few weeks later, his wife had thrown him out, two days before their anniversary and the gifting of the LandJet. I had talked to him often and in depth about my plan to drive across the country and find you, so he offered to sell me the van even though he knew I could never afford such a thing. He was a negotiator though, and said, "You could pay me back slowly or we could probably work something out overnight."

"Overnight? How do you figure?" My hair was in a ponytail and I reached back with both hands to loosen it and stared at him as he stared at my breasts. I'd known since I'd been an intern that he wanted to fuck me. I'd never done anything about it for obvious reasons. Still, he was handsome and already a legend, and there's something alluring about seducing such a man. I was also horny as hell. I hadn't had a boyfriend since you left and had begun getting the most intense sexual urges.

He finished staring at my breasts and said, "There are ways, but I need to know you're a serious buyer first."

When Mom gave me the ultimatum, I called Mr. Pervy and told him I was a serious buyer. He was living in the Lowell Hotel and we arranged to meet there at the bar. I was planning on sleeping with him for the van. I had almost succumbed to his advances many times before, so it didn't really seem that bad, but when I got there I couldn't go through with it. We know a lot of women who either got married or stayed in a shitty marriage for money or, as they like to say, "security," but they're just whores without the business acumen, and I didn't want that label.

25

We had a booth in the corner that was dark and private. The entire bar was dark and private and many a real whore had probably sat in the very seat where I was sitting. Mr. Pervy was sporting a smug expression, so I started off the conversation by saying, "I'm sorry, but I can't have sex with you."

He laughed and shook his head like he'd been splashed with cold water and said, "What? I thought you were here to buy the LandJet."

"Let's just cut to the chase, okay. What's it gonna take?" He'd had plenty of flings with other women in the office who all said he was a serious freak, and when men are that sick they want the fantasy much more than the sex.

With a very straight face he said, "Liza, I'm really not sure where all this is coming from."

I propped my elbows on the table and laced my fingers together. "I work for you, Tim. I know all your moves and I know you know why we're here. I'm leaving tonight with or without the van and I'd like to hit the road ASAP, so make me an offer or tell me goodbye."

Mr. Pervy slapped his palms flat down on the table and said, "The title's upstairs, follow me."

When we got to his room, the paperwork was on his desk. He signed the ownership of the LandJet over to me and said, "There's a razor, a can of shaving cream, a costume, and a lollipop in the bathroom. Shave your pussy, put the costume on, and come out with the sucker in your mouth and I'll give you instructions from there."

In the bathroom I stripped to my underwear and stood in front of the mirror. My bra and panties were a black satin set Mom had given me for my birthday. "Black lingerie," she'd said at the time, "will get you anything you want from a man if you know how to wear it." The bra was padded and the cut of the underwear accentuated the shape of my hips. I looked at the razor and shaving cream and laughed because I'd gotten waxed the day before and had nothing to trim. Then I looked in the brown paper bag holding the costume and was bewildered.

Mr. Pervy knocked on the door and asked, "Have you looked yet?"

"Yes."

"Will you wear it?"

"I'll be right out."

Scurrying sounds abruptly ensued and he yelled, "Turn the lights off before you open the door and don't forget the ears!"

I put the costume on. The fabric was soft, broken in, and had a familiar odor, but when I put the lollipop in my mouth the sweetness overpowered my sense of smell. I opened the door and stepped into the bedroom. The lights were low and it was shadowy where he sat on the couch. I had never worn a Minnie Mouse costume and was unsure how to imitate the Disney character. He told me to take off my skirt and show him my "privates." That was the word he used, privates, like I was some kind of kid or something. Once the skirt was off, he said, "Did you have a good day at school today or were the boys mean to you again?" I didn't answer. Then he said, "Do you like your lollipop? You must be a good girl because only good girls get lollipops."

It was too much. I wasn't going to support that kind of role-playing, so I decided to do the sluttiest, most pornographic adult thing I could think of, and moved the lollipop from my mouth to between my legs. The candy was warm and covered with saliva and I lay on my back and manipulated the hard sugary bulb like a Vegas stripper working for tips at bachelor party. There was no mistaking me for anything other than a full-blown woman, but just to make sure, I moaned like an adult, and when his breathing got faster, I arched my lower back off the ground and popped the lollipop through my butt cheeks into my anus. He gasped and I flipped onto my knees, found him in the dark, and stuck the sucker in his mouth, so that from that moment on, whenever he came he would always be reminded of the taste of my shit.

I stood up and looked at him. The lollipop was clenched in his teeth and he was grinning like a madman. A camera flashed twice and the two explosions of light were blinding. I stepped back into the bathroom, and without the candy in my mouth the smell on the costume returned, and I realized it was the scent of Chanel No. 5.

When I reentered the room all the lights were lit and he was dressed in his business suit and fancy shoes. His room was very clean; his clothes were all put away and the few magazines and books he had were neatly stacked. A half-packed suitcase rested at the foot of his bed. I asked where he was going and he coolly replied, "London."

He handed me two sets of keys and said, "This is our secret, right?"

"Just tell me one thing. What kind of perfume does your wife wear?"

He ran his finger along my cheek. "Not Chanel No. 5, if that's what you're asking."

I quickly stepped away from him. He smiled victoriously and pushed me out the door saying, "Call me from the road. I'll be thinking about you."

Family Portrait

—◦◦◦—

I went straight from the hotel to Pervy's garage and picked up the Land-Jet. The night was getting late and there wasn't much traffic, which was good, because the van was much bigger than any car I'd ever driven before. I considered not taking the van at all. The whole transaction had left me feeling dirty and cheap, and when I saw the vehicle, my first inclination was to smash the windshield. I needed a shower, a shoulder to cry on, and for someone to tell me I wasn't a sex worker, and I needed this person to be Mom. I rolled down every window in the LandJet and opened the sunroof. Still, everything reeked of Chanel No. 5. The scent followed me across the George Washington Bridge and into New Jersey.

I stopped for the night in Hackensack and rested in a dark corner of a public library's parking lot beneath a burnt-out lamppost, lying on the couch in the rear cabin staring up at the ceiling. Thoughts of roadmaps and role-playing raced through my mind at an uncontrollable tempo. Minnie Mouse waved her four-fingered white-gloved hand at me and, in a high-pitched voice, told me to come to Disney World.

Closing my eyes only made the visions come faster. You had been missing for so long, and I could feel myself slipping away, too. I didn't want to lose us both, and I thought if I could just change my environment, everything would be different and somehow the world would feel the same again.

The next morning the LandJet departed southward on Interstate 95. In my possession was my cell phone, the folded and tattered cover of *New York* magazine featuring Lily Durfee, and a white rabbit's foot bought at the first gas station upon entering New Jersey. The good luck charm hung from the rearview mirror to serve as a reminder of all I'd left behind in Manhattan and as a talisman for the road ahead. The gesture was clichéd, which was exactly what I needed: to feel generic and ordinary and like every other normal person in the world.

After driving eight hours it was time to stop. Since green is your favorite color, I chose to rest in Piney Green, North Carolina. I think you even once described the color of Jack's mountain bike as being a "piney green." You suddenly felt nearby. The rabbit's foot was doing its job; you could have been right around the corner. Then I learned there was a second town called Piney Green in North Carolina. The cashier in the rest station where I was fueling up on gasoline and Skittles pointed to a map of the state folded out and flattened beneath the glass top of the counter, saying, "Why'd they go and give two towns the same name in one state is beyond me, but I guess that's why I ain't the Guv'nah."

I lay down on the couch in the back of the LandJet and wondered if the residents of one Piney Green were happy and if the residents of the other Piney Green were sad. I wondered if anyone lived in both towns. The second Piney Green was only a hundred miles south-southeast and situated right on the Atlantic. You always struck me as someone who would choose to live in a coastal town, so I set off. For entertainment I listened to NPR. They were interviewing a woman who'd been sailing five hundred miles off the coast of Florida when her ship had caught fire and sunk. For an entire day she'd drifted alone with only a life preserver, until a giant sea turtle swam beneath her and buoyed her out of the water. Two days later she was rescued by the Coast Guard. The turtle did not swim away until she was safely lifted onto the ship's deck.

Several listeners called in to challenge her story, but she had witnesses, pictures, and a movie deal from Disney as validation. Images of Mom dressed up in a kiddies' Sea Turtle outfit for Mr. Pervy snapped through my thoughts. I could see the stubble beneath her waistline. The LandJet began to stink of Chanel No. 5. I turned the van around and decided to rest somewhere between the two towns of Piney Green, North Carolina.

The radio stayed off the next morning while the LandJet cruised southward. I was hungry. The only thing I'd eaten in the past thirty-six hours were Skittles, a bag of chips, and red Jell-O. Somewhere in South Carolina, I passed a sign for Walterboro, which reminded me of your old boyfriend, Walter, though I couldn't picture his face or remember where and when you used to date him. The name was so familiar, I was convinced that you two were once madly in love. My stomach started doing flips. Walterboro was thirty-seven miles away, so I decided to stop there for lunch. But then I saw a sign for Screvin, Georgia, and it seemed like it was more than just a coincidence to find a town whose name rhymed with your lucky number, so I drove on deciding to have an early dinner instead.

Once in Screvin, I ordered ribs, mashed potatoes, corn bread, and spinach, and literally licked the plate clean. I left a forty percent tip and returned to the couch in the LandJet to lie down and digest for a minute before hitting the road. Six hours later I woke up with the radio still on. The announcers were talking about a cat that had spontaneously exploded. Their theory was that static buildup on the feline's fur had caused the blast. Florida was only hours away. Many of the cars surrounding me had license plates from the Sunshine State. I sat in the driver's seat with my hand on the ignition, frozen with terror that the engine would explode as soon as I turned the key.

Five hours later I pulled over on the side of the highway just outside the city limits of Orlando. Images of Mickey, Minnie, and Goofy were as much a part of the landscape as palm trees and pink flamingos. My airways constricted. The LandJet shook with each passing semi. I looked in the mirror and found spinach stuck to my teeth. I called Jack, and before he could say hello, I asked him what your lucky number was. He told me it was nine. I asked him about the color of his bike. He told me it was blue. I asked him if he remembered your old flame, Walter. He said the name didn't ring a bell.

Then he asked me where I was and if I was all right. Apparently I sounded funny.

"Florida," I told him.

"What are you doing in Florida?"

"You don't remember Walter?"

"There never was a Walter."

"That's fine," I answered, "because I'm going to Disney World!"

Jack tried to say something back, but I had already hung up the phone.

I stayed in the theme park only long enough to pay someone to take a Polaroid of me standing next to Minnie Mouse. With permanent marker I scrawled "Family Portrait" at the bottom of the picture and sent it to Mom.

The Mayor's Daughters

—∿∿—

My doctor is outside the room arguing with Officer Ryan. Doctor Mawji was in my room earlier this morning, which was the first time we met. Initial visits with new doctors are always awkward because I have to go through all my medications with them. What made matters worse this morning was that Officer Ryan was standing at the door listening as I rattled off my list of prescriptions: Lithium, Syraquil, Zyprexa, Remeron, Synthroid, and Lunesta. I was hoping Officer Ryan wouldn't know the difference between Syraquil and Monistat-7, but as we already know, he's on to me. Dr. Mawji just stormed off down the hallway and now Officer Ryan is storming into my room. "There are some people from the station here who want to talk to you, but your doctor won't let them," he says like he's accusing me of a crime.

I pull a page from *Silly Little Rich Girl* and ask, "Which station? CBS or ABC?"

He shakes his head and replies, "Let me tell you something about cops: we got good memories."

I pat my stomach and reply, "Like an elephant."

He grants me a smirk and says, "We train ourselves to remember things like license plates, street addresses, distress codes...and medications. Syraquil and Lithium ain't your run-of-the-mill happy pills, now are they?"

Marcus is standing in the hallway. He peers over his shoulder into the room, but the door is shut and he can't hear anything, even though he's trying to listen.

"How many people know?" Officer Ryan asks.

"How many people know what?"

He tilts his head to the side and smiles condescendingly. "Okay. I'll spell it out for ya. How many people know that you're a fucking psychopath?" He opens his eyes real wide and clucks his head.

"Just me, my brother, and a handful of doctors."

Officer Ryan squeezes his lips to one side and looks around the room. "That's not a lot of people, Liza. That is not a lot of people."

"It's personal."

"I bet."

"I'd like to keep it that way."

He puffs out his cheeks as he nods mulling over the request and then says, "That might be tough. Work with me though and maybe it'll happen."

Officer Ryan walks out of the room, and as soon as he opens the door to the hallway, Marcus walks into the room with news. Lily Durfee's kidnappers have sent a ransom note to the other executive producers of *Silly Little Rich Girl,* demanding they surrender the secret videotapes Lily made by five o'clock this afternoon. But the thing is, Jamie, the EPs didn't even know those tapes existed. No one knew about Lily's films but me.

"Seems kinda fishy," Marcus says. "Most kidnappers send a ransom note to the family and they always ask for money. What do you know about these tapes?"

"Nothing. They were secret."

His eyes challenge me to lie to him again as he sits on the chair by my bed and leans in close. "Whose side do you think I'm on?"

"What sides?"

"There's you," he glances towards the door, "and there's the bloated leprechaun in the hallway. Something's going on between you two, and I can either help you or not."

"I don't know what to say, Marcus." I look over the edge of my bed to make sure my purse is still there in case I need a pill.

Marcus notices and asks, "What's in the bag?"

I could tell him it's filled with anti-anxiety, antipsychotic, and antidepressant medications, but I want him to like me. "I don't know, girl stuff. What's with the third degree?"

Marcus exhales an annoyed breath and walks over to look out the window.

Do you know the bag I'm talking about, Jamie? Maybe you've seen it on

33

TV. It's blue and white leather and it has my initials, LD, on it. The lettering is large, three inches to be exact, the L is blue and on the white section of the bag and the D is white and on the blue section. Lily has the very same purse, which can be confusing since we have the same initials. It seemed odd that she chose to carry the same exact bag as me, but she said it was more eye-catching when we'd show up to events with matching accessories. She was right, too. The blue and white model is our biggest seller.

Lily's smart like that. She wired her entire apartment herself with hidden cameras and recording devices and taught herself the ropes of digital media. No one was allowed in her apartment before signing a release form, and she hung a notice on her door warning those who entered that they may be on camera. Everyone assumed the sign and the waiver were for the TV show, so when they arrived and didn't see fifty crew members standing around, they thought they were safe, unaware of the pinhole camera that was pointed at them, tucked neatly in the seams of the chandelier hanging from the ceiling.

Lily called me to her apartment the afternoon of the night she was kidnapped. I sat in her office watching her transfer files of the most damning footage she'd recorded onto a disk. When she was finished, she said, "My greatest hits," as she dropped the unlabeled disk into the inside pocket of her blue and white handbag, the same interior pocket I use to hide my meds.

Marcus turns the television on and hands me the remote control. The channel is tuned to CNN and they're interviewing a senator from Texas who's trying to ban cheerleading from the high schools in his state because he doesn't approve of the suggestive nature of the dance routines. Marcus casually says, "Sounds like the girls in Texas might be safer if they banned the senator from the pep rallies instead."

I laugh and, now that the ice is broken, say, "If you really want to help me, Marcus, tell me what you know about Officer Ryan."

Marcus lowers his voice and says, "He's been on the force almost thirty years. Used to be in charge of the mayor's security detail until Nine-Eleven when they stopped using NYPD and replaced them with FBI."

"The mayor?" I instantly think of Lily and her hidden cameras. "His daughters were on our show. They used to hang out with Lily."

"Wild children," Marcus says with a knowing look.

I take a deep breath and reply, "I think I'm going to need your help."

Marcus looks at me and there's wisdom in his eyes. He's smart enough to know that my trouble with Officer Ryan might involve the mayor's daughters, and he's also smart enough to know that there's probably nothing he can do to help me.

Lily nicknamed the mayor's daughters "the MDs." The press follows them as closely as they do Lily, because their dad is Henry Brownback, who after serving for two years as a conservative liberal "found God" and quickly became the frontrunner for the Republican Party's presidential nomination. But not everyone in the Brownback family shares the same values, and as the mayor's stances veered rightward, the MDs' antics grew wilder.

When the mayor attended a pro-life dinner at the Pierre Hotel, the MDs were photographed getting out of a limousine wearing short skirts and no underwear. When the mayor went to Washington to meet with the president about banning stem-cell research, the MDs were modeling French lingerie at Fashion Week in Milan. When the mayor pledged to tighten our borders, the MDs got arrested in Cancun for public intoxication. A speech against gay marriage sent them dirty dancing into a lesbian nightclub.

And it went on, classic passive-aggressive behavior from two girls who just wanted their father to love them as much as he loved his work. By the time they bumped and grinded their way into Lily's net, they were strung out at the end of a very public rope. "Easy pickin's," is how Lily described them right before they arrived for what would soon become a legendary poker night at Lily's apartment.

Thinking about the MDs sends my thoughts to you, Jamie. They fought for their father's attention by acting immature and irresponsible. You fought for Mom's affection by removing yourself from her completely. Both situations are sad, one very public, the other spookily private. In the end, it's still the same old story of how far a child will go to win a parent's love.

Holly

—⁓—

When I arrived in St. Petersburg the first order of business was taking a shower. So I found a recreation center located one block from a cluster of retirement homes, which provided the bulk of its clientele. The hours were from eight in the morning to eight at night, and every Tuesday, Thursday, and Saturday there was bingo at four o'clock. For five dollars a day, full access was granted to the indoor swimming pool, reading room, shuffleboard court, and most importantly, the women's locker room.

I had no clothes except for what was on my back, so I went to Marshalls and bought some shorts and T-shirts, a bathing suit, toiletries, a pillow, sheet, and a blanket for the couch in the LandJet. I had a small bedroom in the back of the van and a large bathroom in the locker room of the rec center. I had a black one-piece Speedo that made me look thin. I had no closet full of clothes to contemplate every morning, no risk arbitrage, no social engagements, and only one pair of shoes, New Balance sneakers to be exact. And I had bingo three days a week. Life had never been so simple.

My strategy was to get a job in a place with lots of foot traffic and work as many hours as possible hoping that you would pass by. One by one, I visited all the major supermarkets filling out applications to be a grocery bagger, but no one would hire me because I didn't have a home address or local phone number. One man was almost willing to give me a job. He was about thirty years old and had acne scars all over his neck. The interview went well until he invited me to a club and asked if I did ecstasy. When I said no, he held my application to my face and ripped it in half.

Meanwhile, Martha-Ray, the overseer of the rec center, was on to me. Even though I wore a one-piece Speedo and swam laps every morning, she saw me for what I truly was, a vagabond living in a van outside. There was someone else who swam laps every morning, and after passing each other in the pool and the locker room four days in a row, she finally broke the ice and spoke. Her name was Holly, a sinewy woman with short black hair and mysterious green eyes. She was attractive, in her late forties, and came across as wise. She struck me as the kind of person I would turn to if I found myself on a sinking ship looking for the fastest way out.

Holly first spoke to me in the locker room. We had both finished swimming and I had unknowingly picked the locker next to hers. She was standing there in her bathing suit when I emerged from the shower wrapped in a towel.

"Sorry," I said, stopping short when I saw her. "I didn't mean to crowd you."

"Wouldn't you know it? We're the only two people in here and we're practically on top of each other." She smiled and stepped aside to make room, peeling off her wet bathing suit. "You're a good swimmer," she said, standing naked in front of me.

I thanked her and noticed a long jagged scar running up the left side of her body from her hip to her armpit. She saw me glance at it and joked, "I used to be in a rough line of work," as she placed her suit in a clear plastic bag.

I chuckled and undraped my towel because she seemed so comfortable in her nudeness that I felt uncomfortable not being naked. "I used to work for an investment banker." I pointed to my head. "All my scars are up here."

Holly laughed. "Spend the morning with me. You are new here and there are things you should see." It didn't matter that she was a stranger and we were both naked and alone in a locker room. All that mattered was the look in her eyes and instinct told me to trust her.

Holly took me to downtown St. Petersburg and gave me a tour of the Salvador Dali Museum. Then we rode a teal-colored trolley through the museum district. The day was overcast and breezy and few people were out. Holly hopped off the back of the trolley before it came to a complete stop and shouted, "Follow me!"

In her car, a hybrid Toyota Prius, we drove out to the Pinellas County incinerator. She spotted a wood stork, which she said was endangered, and then pointed out a bright pink roseate spoonbill as it swooped down from a branch overhead and skidded along the surface of the storm water storage area. "The incinerator warms the water," Holly said, "which attracts insects and fish. That's why all these fabulous birds come here—to eat."

For a long time neither of us spoke. Jumping fish, rippling water, and squawking birds were our symphony, backed by the steady hum of the burning incinerator. Birds of all different colors and sizes came and went. Some would dive beak first into the water and completely submerge themselves before exploding into the air with a fish clenched firmly in their mouths.

When Holly dropped me off at the rec center later, she got out of her car and circled the LandJet with a scrutinizing eye. My bathing suit, now dry, hung from the side-view mirror. She opened the rear door and saw the couch still made up with the sheets and the pillow.

"Is this where you're living?" It was the first personal question she had asked all day.

"It's actually very comfortable."

"Get in your van and follow me. You're staying at my house tonight." She spun on her heels and hopped in her Prius, leaving me no time to respond.

I followed Holly out of the parking lot knowing it was dangerous, but hoped that somehow she would lead me to you. We drove nearly half an hour, first over a long suspension bridge towards Tampa and then northward on a quiet two-lane road shouldering the coastline. A tall hedge of waxy leaves and vine branches lined the roadside. After seventeen miles, Holly pulled over at a small break in the foliage. A dirt road led to a steel gate that was once painted Army green but had since faded. Holly unhooked the catch, swung open the entrance, and bowed with a twirl of her arm.

The LandJet shuddered and bobbed as it crossed a set of train tracks that ran parallel to the property. The dirt path was barely wide enough to accommodate the van and lined with thick brush and felled trees. There was no room to pull over and let Holly pass, so I drove forward until the winding lane opened up to a great lawn that gradually led down to a peninsula beach with Tampa Bay on one side and the Gulf of Mexico on the other.

Holly parked next to me. It was dusk and both our headlights were on, their beams of light extending across the lawn and dispersing above the water. Tiny insects swarmed in the glowing air and I watched their in-flight dance hypnotized until Holly broke the spell by knocking on the van's window.

"Your bungalow is just down that path," she said, pointing to a walkway leading into a grove of pine trees near the water.

I got out of the van and said, "I'm sorry, but I don't think I can stay."

"Don't be silly, it's no trouble at all."

"That's not it."

"I promise you'll be a lot safer here than sleeping in a van on the street. That's why I invited you; for your safety."

I contemplated this. "What's the rent?"

"Well, for starters: happiness."

"I'm afraid I don't have that kind of coin."

"Of course you do. And you don't even need to find your sister to access the great wealth inside of you."

Then everything turned dark and the earth opened up beneath my feet.

When I regained consciousness, I'd been moved from the LandJet to a bungalow. Holly was sitting in the corner reading and lifted her head when she heard me rustling on the bed. The room was a sparse square with a small bathroom in the corner shielded by only a curtain. The floor was wooden and recently sanded and polished. The walls had a fresh coat of white paint, and two windows had been installed but their trim had not been stained yet. Holly sat in a chair painted a Mediterranean blue at a matching table upon which my few belongings had been stacked.

"I didn't mean to stun you," Holly said. "It was senseless of me to be so careless."

"How do you know about my sister?"

"I recognized you from the news. CNBC reported your sister's disappearance because your mother is such a well-known business woman."

I propped myself up on some pillows and said, "That was a long time ago."

"About eight months."

"Exactly eight months."

She placed her book on the table. "I remember watching you."

"You remember that?"

"You were wearing a blue skirt and a long-sleeved button-down shirt

39

that was the same color. The woman standing in front of you was wearing a short black skirt, black boots, and a white short-sleeved shirt." She showed just a hint of a smile. "I have an eidetic memory. I knew who you were the first day I saw you."

I recalled the tour she'd given me at the Dali museum, how she'd known every date and detail about each painting. I thought of the incinerator and her familiarity with the various bird species. She even remembered the PR witch's boots.

"So, are you some kind of genius or something?" I asked.

She smiled and stood up. "Let's have something to eat. It's getting late."

Outside it had begun to drizzle. The day's grayness had finally won and the atmosphere succumbed to the pressure system that had been promising rain. I followed Holly along a curvy path that took us from the grove of trees housing my bungalow across a lawn and into another grove of trees. A system of paths led to various barracks and outbuildings. Burning torches lined the walkways and lit our course through grounds that looked like they'd been well maintained at one time, but were now overgrown. Holly walked to the largest building at the center of the compound and opened a screen door to a large kitchen.

On one side of the room was a long wooden table with a bench on each side for seating. On the other side of the room was an island with a metal countertop that housed a cutting board and a deep sink above an old dishwasher. All the appliances were very old and industrial. Holly opened the refrigerator's big swinging door, pulled out a bowl of pesto pasta and a roasted chicken, and made me a plate.

I looked around. "This is a really cool place."

"Thanks. It used to belong to Uncle Sam. In fact, the land we're on is just a small piece of what was once an air force base. I bought it in an auction and then, when they looked into my finances, they realized I'd never paid any taxes." She laughed at herself. "You either have to be extremely cocky or extremely stupid to be in my old line of work and buy something from the government." She shook her head. "I was both."

"What did you do?"

"Count cards. It's good work if you can get it. The funny thing is, once I came clean rather than arrest or fine me, they told me they'd let me off if I did some 'consulting' for them. So here we are."

"What kind of consulting?"

Her eyes twinkled and she replied, "Espionage."

I laughed and she was laughing, too. "Forgive me, but you're a total hippy. How the hell were you a spy?"

"Well, I didn't get in any car chases or wear a phony mustache if that's what you mean, but I did study some amazing satellite images and cracked a few codes that actually helped catch a *real* spy according to your definition."

"If that's true then that's amazing," I said.

She shrugged and didn't try to make me believe her. "Now I've got two shows on the Home Shopping Network. One sells a line of jewelry I design, and the other sells the gems and ornaments that form my jewelry, along with a manual on how to make it at home."

"That's really cool. I want to be a designer too, so it's nice to see it's actually possible to make money at it."

"I do okay." She shrugged again and I liked her modesty. "And hey, when times get hard I just take a quick trip to Vegas." She was grinning but not kidding.

"It's good work if you can get it." I said, realizing I was sitting on an old military bench at an old military table across from an ex-spy on land tendered for espionage. I don't know why, but I thought of Mom. I wanted her next to me. I wanted her to meet Holly and I wanted to be the one to introduce them. Basically, I wanted her to be proud of me for befriending such an interesting person. Then I realized we'd never outrun the fact that she is our mother and that we are her daughters, and for a second I thought it might be cruel to find you now that you were free.

Smoke and Mirrors

—⁓—

The next day I walked the edge of the property, following the train tracks in each direction. The hedge was too high to look over and when I parted the branches to create a peephole, I found a chainlink fence camouflaged by the shrubbery. Every few hundred yards, old rusty signs hung that read: PRIVATE PROPERTY – FEDERAL LAND – TRESSPASSERS WILL BE PROSECUTED. It wasn't much later than six in the morning. I'd been awake since four.

When I returned, I saw a figure at the end of the driveway dressed in a HAZMAT suit, so I hid behind a tree trunk wondering if I had spent the night sleeping on land contaminated by uranium or plutonium. Had Holly chosen me to be an unwitting player in a government science experiment? Had a chip been planted beneath my skin overnight? Would I be followed and abducted for yearly follow-ups for the rest of my now shortened life? This is your brain on paranoia. The figure in the white suit took off the hat and waved for me to come out from behind the tree. It was Holly. As I got closer, I realized the HAZMAT suit was actually just a pair of white overalls, a white canvas shirt, and a white bonnet with a screen tucked into her clothing. She told me to go to my bungalow and change into the gear on my bed and meet her by the water.

The gear on my bed was the same beekeeping garb Holly wore, plus a roll of tape and a note saying, "Tape closed all loose openings!" When I got to the beach, Holly was holding a gadget that looked like a thermos with a miniature accordion attached. She pumped it to billow smoke into a thin horizontal vent stretching across the entire width of a large, square wooden box. Holly calmly and methodically took the top off the box, puffed it with smoke, removed a shelf from the box, puffed it with smoke, examined the shelf, puffed the box with smoke, put the shelf back, and puffed in more smoke. She didn't use a lot of smoke and all her movements were slow and fluid. I watched her check five shelves and not once did a bee fly from the hive.

Holly had six Langstrop hives—wooden boxes with vertical shelves. She waved me over and handed me the smoker. "Use a little bit and keep your heart rate down. Bees can sense stress hormones in your body, and if they don't like it, they'll release a pheromone that tells all the other bees to attack."

"That's not really helping," I said as I billowed a puff through the bottom vent.

"Good. Now take the top off real slow and hit 'em with smoke again. The smoke calms them down, but if you use too much, it can kill them."

I followed her exact steps from the previous hive, and she examined each shelf, or "cell" as she called them, for drones, partially developed bees that die and take up space that could be filled with honey. You'd think I'd get nervous handling bees for the first time, but the precise and methodical nature of the work was actually quite therapeutic and slowed my thoughts. We took turns with the remaining hives and afterwards sat on the lawn and looked out over the water. "That was amazing," I said. "Thanks for letting me do that."

"You're a natural."

"This is a really beautiful place, Holly. Thanks for letting me spend the night and being so nice. I doubt I'll ever tend a beehive again in my life."

"We're taping the shows for our newest jewelry line in a month and I need to hire a model to be my onstage assistant. Do you have any interest?"

"Me?"

Holly laughed. "Yeah, it's easy. You just stand there and smile."

"I'm not sure I'm staying in Florida that long." I explained my theory behind the *New York* article and how St. Petersburg was my first stop. I wondered if you ever watched the Home Shopping Network, Jamie. I tried to imagine you sitting in an air-conditioned living room sipping a sugary iced tea and shopping by phone. The scenario seemed entirely possible.

"Did you like your room?" Holly asked. "I've been fixing it up because I'm thinking about hiring a caretaker. I'm traveling a lot and the jewelry show is taking up more of my time, so I can't keep up with this place the way I used to. I'm leaving tomorrow for three weeks, and in about ten to fifteen days those hives are going to be at full capacity, and if someone doesn't harvest the honey and make room for new cells, those bees are gonna swarm and I'll never see them again."

"Swarm?"

"Yeah. Once they run out of room they have to find somewhere else to live. Think you can handle it? It's pretty simple. You just do what we did today, except rather than putting the cells back, you crush them in a big metal bowl and let it sit in the sun for a while so the honey gets warm and runny, and then you strain the mush through cheesecloth into a bucket and jar up the good stuff. It'll only take a few hours to do one hive a day and you can spend the rest of the time looking for Jamie." Then she pointed at a twenty-foot by twenty-foot section of the lawn that was staked out and explained her plans to plant a garden. She said I could stay even longer if I helped build the fence and that she had enough odd jobs to board me for several months.

We shook on it and then she said she had to visit a friend at the DMV and suggested I come. She brought a jar of honey, a long pair of tweezers, and a small plastic box with three bees in it. There was a long line, which we bypassed after Holly flashed her ID to a clerk, who lifted up the hinged counter he stood behind and escorted us to a backroom. A black man in his fifties named Floyd waved us to his desk. Holly gave him the jar of honey and said, "Let's see those knuckles," as she grabbed his hand and lifted it towards her face to examine.

"It just keeps getting worse," Floyd said, eyeing the plastic box with the three yellow jackets. "Let's get this over with."

Holly kissed one of his knuckles, pulled a bee out with the tweezers, and held it to Floyd's swollen finger joint until it stung him. "It's for his arthritis," she explained to me. "Bee venom stimulates the anti-inflammatory process and the immune system." Holly stung the three longest fingers on Floyd's left hand and asked him to do a search for people with the last name Davis living in the St. Petersburg area. He found seventeen. She asked him to narrow it down to first names beginning with J. He found one: Jerome Davis, age forty-four, organ donor. Holly patted my knee and said, "I thought it was worth a try." Then she said to Floyd, "My friend here needs to register her new car and she probably needs insurance, too. Put her on Gov Plan 89H and list her at my address."

Floyd asked me for basic information as he typed with one hand. About three months later, I got arrested in Idaho and found out the van was never registered or insured and there was no such thing as "Gov Plan 89H." The lingo was nothing but gobbledygook—part of Holly's sham—so there really isn't that much space to cross from paranoia to gullibility.

The next stop was a supermarket, because Holly needed gum and magazines. I entered the store with a gambler's optimism that you'd be there. This was Holly's aim all along, to bring me on a mini search expedition. She could have bought her sundries at a gas station, but instead chose the biggest and busiest supermarket in the area.

I left Holly in the magazine section and began a methodical sweep from the cosmetics aisle on the left side of the building all the way to the right side of the store where fresh produce was sold. On my second lap I grabbed a cart so people wouldn't think I was wandering aimlessly. On my third lap I started putting groceries in the basket because people were looking at me funny and I wanted them to stop.

Holly found me on my fourth lap. My cart was filled with two cases of bottled water, ten boxes of low-fat Wheat Thins, three jumbo packs of peanut M&M's, and a tub of chocolate frosting. Holly looked at my items and raised her eyebrows.

"I don't know what came over me." I tried to laugh it off. "Sometimes I get the most intense cravings for the strangest foods."

Holly was kind enough to spend the rest of the day showing me around town; I think she wanted to spend a little more time with me before leaving her compound in my trust. She was vetting me, which is ironic considering what happened, but that day she showed me how to get to the library, the Tampa Humane Society, the homeless shelter, the church with the busiest soup kitchen, and a natural foods store, because they were all places I planned on checking for you regularly. Holly even waited in her car as I ran into each stop with your picture to see if you'd been spotted. You hadn't, although the clerk at the natural foods store said you looked familiar, but I'm pretty sure he was baked.

On our way home, I made Holly drive across town to a fabric warehouse where I bought a used sewing machine and several yards of sage brushed canvas and treated leather. The warehouse was in a sketchy part of town at the end of an alley filled with abandoned dumpsters. Holly wasn't happy about being there, but she navigated the potholes and curbs in the streets

45

like she had driven them before, and when we drove past a man smoking a cigarette on a stoop, he waved to her and she pretended not to notice him.

Later that night, Holly came to my bungalow as I was getting ready for bed. She caught me in the same black lingerie I had worn for Mr. Pervy. I'd been so horny for so long, I'd begun hanging out in sexy outfits because it was arousing. I actually drove the entire stretch of the Tam Miami Trail in nothing more than a tank top and black stockings. She had already seen me naked, so I didn't think finding me in my underwear would freak her out. When I opened the door she was a bit taken aback and asked, "Am I coming at a bad time?"

"Sorry," I said. "Do you want to come in?"

Holly looked at me from head to toe. "Is everything okay, Liza?"

"Of course!" I shouted, but didn't mean to. "Why?"

"Ever since we left the DMV you've seemed a little off, and to be honest, I'm feeling nervous about leaving you here alone."

"I feel great, Holly. I've never had more energy in my life, and I think it's because I'm finally looking for Jamie." I put my shirt on and sat on the bed, and Holly seemed a little more comfortable.

"I need you to do a few things for me while I'm gone," she said.

"Sure. Anything."

"I'd like you to call your mom and tell her you're okay."

"My mom?"

"I'm sure she's worried about you, and I don't want any police or hired private eyes coming to my property looking for a runaway."

"I'm twenty-two years old! I can go wherever I want."

"Just, please, okay?"

"Sure."

"The other thing is, the day before I get back, a friend of mine is boating through on his way from Jacksonville to Key West and I packed him fifty jars of honey to sell in his health food shop down there." Holly slid a crate into my room. "Do you mind giving this to him when he stops by?"

"Not at all."

"Thanks. His boat is too big to dock, so you'll have to row out a little to give it to him. He said he's planning on getting here about an hour after sunset." The crate was wooden, very sturdy, and the shape and size of a case of beer bottles. The lid was nailed shut. "You might want to leave it in your van until he comes so you don't forget."

"Okay," I said. "Good idea."

Then she asked for a picture of you to take on her trip. She said she'd show it to as many people as possible and put it on her display table at trade shows. I gave her the shot of you standing in front of the reservoir in Central Park. I took that picture a week before you vanished. It's barely even in focus.

The Swarm

———

"What are you calling here for?" This was how Mom answered the phone when I called her later that night. "He showed me the picture of you, Liza. Now I know why you liked your job so much. Then I get the picture you sent from Disney World, and by this point all I want to know is what I did to deserve such treatment?"

I took a deep breath and calmly began: "I'm sorry, Mom. I didn't know you were having an affair with him until after he made me put on that stupid costume."

Mom cut me off saying, "Tim didn't make you do anything, Liza. He said you delivered some papers from his office, and when you saw the costume, you snuck it into the bathroom and put it on without his knowing."

"Why would I do that?"

"He said you pinned him against his bed and took a picture of the two of you with your cell phone, and said if he didn't give you the van, you'd show me the picture."

"And you believe him? That's the dumbest story I've ever heard!"

Mom sighed loudly. "Liza, all I know is that Tim has a picture of you naked from the waist down wearing a Minnie Mouse costume, so something somewhere clearly went awry."

"I'm not the first Davis woman to wear that costume, am I, Mom? You know Mr. Pervy was the one who told me to call CNBC about Jamie, and then he shorted your stock. That's, like, practically illegal. The guy's a psychopath. Why else would he show you that picture? Why would he even take the picture in the first place, Mom?"

Mom took a moment to catch her breath. After some silence, she said, "Honey, you need to figure out whatever it is you're going through, and when you decide you want help, give me a call, but until then it's best if you stay away because I can't support this kind of behavior."

"How was London?"

"I'm going to hang up now, Liza."

"I bet he didn't show you the picture until you guys got home, did he?"

"This is exactly why you need to stop calling me."

"By the way, you might not want to kiss him on the mouth ever again."

"Goodbye Liza." Mom hung up and I fell to the floor and cradled my phone like it was her body, like it was your body, and at some point in the middle of the night I called her back, but the line had been disconnected.

I woke up the next morning and crawled to the bathroom to pee. My hair was tangled, my mouth sour, and my eyes were bloodshot and scratchy. I didn't have the energy to flush the toilet or even pull my underwear all the way up. I saw myself in the mirror and began to cry, and then I threw up into the unflushed toilet, which sent my urine and vomit splashing against my face.

Not until nine o'clock that night did I get out of bed. Full choruses of little girls were singing the nursery rhyme from underneath the floor of the bungalow, so I began the sketches for the canvas and leather totes and got my silence back. For the next four days the chorus would come and I'd sew till it was quiet. On the fifth day I walked the train tracks running alongside the property. When I found a secluded area hidden from the road, I lay down across the rails and waited. A train never came.

On the sixth day the chorus resumed and I finished sewing the first bag.

By the seventh day I had drunk six bottles of water and eaten two boxes of Wheat Thins. I hadn't searched for you once and just looking at the LandJet made me nauseous.

On the eighth day I rowed a hundred yards offshore and sank the black lingerie and all my sexy undergarments in a canvas sack.

On the ninth day I realized I had no underwear.

On the twelfth day I ate nothing but M&M's dipped in chocolate frosting.

On the thirteenth day I wasn't hungry.

On the fourteenth day I made my bed and spent the afternoon sitting on the doorstep of the bungalow thinking about all the different ways I could kill myself. When it was dark I walked down to the beach and stared at the lights of St. Petersburg twinkling across the water. I yelled your name and didn't hear an echo, so I waded into the water up to my neck. I tried to fall asleep like this, hoping the tide would rise and cover me. A crab scuttled over my foot and I shrieked and swam back to shore. This small moment of fear was the first emotion other than despair that I had felt in two weeks. My heart was pounding, my hands were shaking, and I started to laugh uncontrollably because I knew I had returned from wherever I had been for the past fourteen days.

The next morning I rose at sunrise and taped myself into the overalls and screened bonnet and harvested the first hive's honey. The work immediately put my mind at ease and the repetitive nature of the task reminded me of sewing, which is probably why it felt like I'd been doing it my whole life. For five days I harvested in the morning and sewed in the afternoons, and by the last day, all the canvas totes with leather straps and piping were finished. I got to the final hive late that morning and was expecting the bees to be harder to control, but when I lifted the lid, the hive was empty except for a few dead bees at the bottom of the box. The cells were full of honey but the bees had swarmed.

I looked out over the water for a moving cloud of insects and checked under the hives in case the entire five-thousand-strong troupe was hiding as a joke, and that's when I noticed the homemade shelves nailed to the bottom of the Langstrop boxes. When I opened one, I found bricks of money wrapped in thick plastic and duct tape. Three of the six hives' secret shelves were empty, and I realized that the crate in the LandJet was probably not filled with honey at all.

I had to laugh. Holly didn't need me to tend to her hives, she needed me to make a drop, and she'd wanted to store the money in my car just in case there was a last-minute raid. That night when the boat came many hours after sunset, I rowed the crate out, and a man threw me a line so I could dock at his stern. He was wearing a baseball hat, a dark turtleneck, and sunglasses—at two in the morning. I took one look at him and said, "Put your hands up!"

He laughed and said, "Come on, sweetie. I can't be idling here all night."

I fell asleep later thinking how in my short search for you I had already visited the fringes of prostitution and money laundering, but somehow it all felt right, and when I woke up the next morning, I was convinced you were alive and somewhere around the next corner. Then there was a knock at the door, and when I answered, you were standing right in front of me. So I fainted.

Your Twin

—⁓—

Obviously it wasn't you, Jamie. Holly was home and toting a life-sized mannequin that she had had made to look like your twin. She instantly realized what she had done and rushed to my side apologizing profusely, explaining she'd used the picture of you to make four models as props for her show. Millions of people watch the Home Shopping Network and she thought someone might recognize you and call the number on the screen with information. Her gesture was heartfelt and not intended as a cruel prank. I forgave her and looked you over. She had dressed you in khaki pants and a blue-collared shirt. The blonde wig was woven into pigtails, just like your hair.

"One of your hives swarmed but they left behind a bunch of money," I told her. "So I sent it to my bank in New York. I hope that's okay. I mean, finders, keepers, right?"

Holly smiled. "You're not after money, you're after something else. That's why I picked you in the first place."

I looked at the mannequin and your resemblance was uncanny. Holly must have had to pay a lot extra to have the job rushed, and she did it out of the kindness of her sneaky, illicit heart. She even gave you pigtails, Jamie. How could I stay mad at her? She was right, too—I wasn't after her money, but I did want the exposure on the HSN. I wanted my search for you out on the airwaves, and to hawk my totes on her show, so I told her I'd hidden the money and listed my demands. I was bluffing and she probably knew, but I think she really did feel badly, so she agreed. Once we settled, I said, "I'm sorry your bees swarmed."

"It happens. They either get fed up and leave or they all die from a mite infestation. The mites are a real problem."

"But if they all died wouldn't we find them in the hive?" I asked.

"No. They fly away, then they die."

"So you never really know if they swarmed or if they died?"

Holly shook her head. She knew exactly what I was thinking about.

"It'd be nice to know, wouldn't it?" I asked her.

She took me in her arms, patted my back, and instructed me to follow her to the lawn where she pointed at a shovel and a pair of work gloves near the fence line for the garden. "Start digging," she said. "Manual labor is penicillin for the soul."

It was only morning, but the day was promising a muggy heat with a thickness in the air that made me sweat within minutes, so I went back to the bungalow to change into my black one-piece bathing suit. Your twin was sitting in the chair waiting patiently, and I kissed your cheek and drew a peace sign on the bottom of your left foot before heading back to the garden.

Holly instructed me to dig a hole a foot in diameter and three feet deep at each of the four corner posts. With each break of the earth came a renewed sense that the past was behind me and the future bright. The simple, repetitive physical action of jabbing the shovel into the ground and scooping out dirt set my mind on cruise control, and for a while, there was nothing to think about except moving soil. As I was finishing the fourth and final hole, my shovel collided with a hard metal object that was immovable and much larger than the foot-wide opening I had made, so I called for Holly before digging up any more of her lawn. "Don't you think it's strange?" I asked her.

"Very," she said.

I wiped soil and sweat off my forehead and got down on one knee to look deeper in the hole. "This used to be an air force base, right? What if this is an old bomb or a missile that fell off one of the planes?"

Holly tapped the mystery metal. "The runway and hangars were a mile north of here. This land was just scrub. I promise there's nothing dangerous under our feet."

"Well, what would you like me to do?" I peered deep into the hole again.

She shrugged and said, "Keep digging."

The Night with the Mayor's Daughters

—ᴧᴧ—

Officer Ryan is looking for clues as well. He just entered my room and grabbed my purse from the floor next to me.

"What are you doing?" I ask him.

"I did my homework. Lithium is for manic-depressives and Seroquel is an antipsychotic. You're on both, so that's a double-whammy."

"Double-whammy? You should be a doctor."

"I like being a cop just fine, thanks."

"That's probably for the best, what with doctors having to be so smart and all."

Officer Ryan places the purse on a windowsill out of reach, and says, "My chief and two lieutenants are coming to talk to you, and I can't have you all drugged up because you don't want to be sad for one minute." He puts on a frowny face.

I frown back at him and ask, "Do they work for the mayor, too? Because I was there that night." I pause to let him comment but he's actually stunned, "Yeah, *that* night," I say. "The night with the mayor's daughters."

The night I'm referring to happened one month ago in the living room of Lily's apartment in plain view of her many hidden cameras. It was a Saturday night, though the exact time of the event is unknown because Lily covered all the clocks with tinfoil and collected her guests' watches at the door like a parent collecting teenagers' car keys when they arrive for a party.

The MDs came over to play poker with Lily and her other guests, including a shortstop from the New York Yankees, the catcher from the New York Mets, a rap star, a playmate turned megastar, me, the Oscar winner for Best Supporting Actor, and two strippers in lingerie who were passing out drinks and loose tabs of ecstasy.

I know it was past 2:00 a.m. because the shortstop for the Yankees ran out of cash and threw his Rolex in the pot as collateral. Lily had me collect the timepiece from her bedroom and wrap it in tinfoil before bringing it to the table. Everyone was drunk and fuzzy from tequila and ecstasy. The strippers, Misty and Memphis, had shed their tops and circled the table in nothing but high heels, black stockings, and panties. I thought I was the only sober person until I accidentally sipped Lily's drink and tasted the apple juice. She saw me holding her glass and said, "Smooth tequila, isn't it?"

"Very," I answered, wondering where she spat out all the hits of ecstasy she had pretended to swallow.

She winked and clicked the stereo's remote control, blasting the attending rapper's hit song. Misty and Memphis began dancing around the table. The Playboy cover girl grabbed the actor to dance, and the baseball players paired off with the MDs. Misty and Memphis flanked the rapper and tore his shirt off as he lip-synched his song, and Lily pulled me from my seat and shimmied behind me.

Everyone was dancing and rubbing their hands all over each other. Lily rested her arms atop my shoulders, leaned into me from behind, and asked, "Do I have your back tonight?"

I swayed in time with her hips and replied, "That depends."

"I'm going to kiss you in a minute. Pretend it's real." She spun me around and planted her lips over mine, covering our faces with her hands to hide the fact that our kiss was as fake as the breasts on Misty and Memphis.

When the song ended, we all sat back in our original seats, but the night had taken an irretrievable turn towards the erotic. More poker was played and the conversation circled around the topic of sex. The rapper admitted to having three children with three different women, or as he referred to them, his babies' mommas. The catcher asked if he'd ever heard of condoms, and one of the MDs suggested abortion.

Sober and keen on her agenda, Lily joked that the girls' father wouldn't approve of such words, and the daughter replied slyly, "Don't be so sure."

55

"What do you mean?" I asked, aiding and abetting.

The MDs looked at each other, conversed in mental sister-speak of eye contact and facial expressions, and then one shrugged and the other one began: "My mother got pregnant when she was forty-six. We weren't supposed to know, but we found the pregnancy test in her bathroom when we were raiding her makeup. She caught us reading the positive result and shouted for our father. When the conversation was over we had a new car to share and our mother was packing for a two-week vacation. She never sent a postcard and we never asked her where she went. Needless to say, we don't have any other siblings." She punctuated her story by biting her lower lip and raising her eyebrows.

The table was silent; even Misty and Memphis were taken aback.

"But your dad is so pro-life," Lily said.

This time the other daughter spoke. Her words were laced with bitterness. "No, he just pretends to be because he wants to be president."

The rapper, whose virility had sparked this conversation, felt obliged to say something, so he added with pride, "I take care of my kids!"

The baseball players exchanged glances before bursting into laughter, and soon enough, Misty and Memphis were pouring drinks and Lily grabbed the deck of cards announcing we were moving on to strip poker.

I don't know how she did it, she must have been dealing from the bottom of the deck, because I almost never lost a hand and the only article of clothing I was forced to shed was a shirt, which was fine, because I was wearing my most flattering bra thanks to Lily's fashion advice earlier in the day.

Strip poker turned into sex poker, and by the end of the night, the MDs had kissed everyone at the table except me. They played as a team and thus had to pay their bets as a team, and I don't think I'll ever erase the image of them sandwiching the rapper's muscular and tattooed body while he stuck his tongue in one sister's mouth as his hands simultaneously groped the bare breasts of the other.

As the game progressed, it became obvious, though never said, that everyone at the table was playing against the MDs. Even Misty and Memphis clued into the gag and poured the MDs drinks as soon as their glasses were empty. By the end of the game the two girls were the only naked people at the table, and when they lost the final hand, they were forced to kiss each other for thirty seconds without stopping, but no one had a watch and the clocks were covered in tinfoil, so we all counted "One Mississippi, two Mississippi," and so on in a slow chant. The atmosphere became tribal and the MDs' drunken ecstasy trip keyed them into this carnal vibe, removing them even farther from reality, and they didn't stop their frantic embrace until we had reached ninety-seven Mississippi.

That was a month ago. Two days after that night, the MDs checked into a drug and alcohol rehabilitation center somewhere in the hills of Pennsylvania. The mayor asked the media and public to respect his daughters' privacy as they navigated the troubled waters as a family.

The girls left rehab only a few days ago. They held a press conference wearing turtlenecks and long pants. They spoke about Jesus and how their faith had helped lead them to a new, more righteous path. I watched them on a television in Lily's apartment. Lily was on her computer editing her recordings. She couldn't see the TV but was listening. When the press conference ended, she didn't even look up from her monitor. She just called over her shoulder, "This could get interesting..."

The Wing

—⁓—

My final days in St. Petersburg could also be described as "interesting." I slept about three hours a night and had more energy than a puppy on a morning walk. Holly and I had finished filming her jewelry workshops on the Home Shopping Network, and what was supposed to have been four days of production stretched into three weeks. The work always came in spurts, so we were either hurrying up or waiting. I didn't mind the waiting. The HSN facility is half a million square feet on fifty-three acres and four and a half thousand people work there on any given day. I know this because I took a tour one afternoon when the crew was changing the set to make it look like we were filming on a new day. I liked it best when in the morning I would be wearing a pant suit and my hair would be pinned up, and in the afternoon my wardrobe would be a dress with my hair let down. It felt like time traveling. Often the Liza in the afternoon felt different from the Liza in the morning.

What I didn't like was being on set. There was always a lot of crew, and even though Holly was under the spotlight, just being her backdrop was too much attention. The lights were bright and hot, and between shoots everyone would shout and equipment would swing overhead and cameras would roll on trolleys across the stage.

Holly held up her end of the deal for spreading the word you were missing and selling my bags. Before the shows aired, she sent out a press release that said Liza Davis, model and couture handbag designer, would be a guest on her show while visiting Florida searching for her missing sister, Jamie Davis. None of the papers picked it up and it's possible B-Global used their muscle to bury the story. It's also possible no one cared but me.

Holly also mentioned you on the air many times. She was good on camera and could talk and talk and sell and sell. Each one of your mannequins was holding a canvas tote, and Holly told viewers to call my cell phone if they had information on your disappearance or were interested in the bags. The bags sold out the first night and not one person knew where you were.

When filming was over, it was a relief to get back to unearthing the mysterious object we'd found in Holly's garden. But my digging didn't last very long. Instead, I decided to paint your portrait on both sides of the LandJet. So I went online and took a course on how to paint using the grid system. The classes weren't hard, didn't take long, and included special software that did the calculations for converting the four-by-six-inch picture of you into a three-by-five-foot replica.

A forty-one-piece spray gun kit was purchased along with enamels, latex, primer, urethane, and several different brushes and nozzles. I also bought five twelve-foot tarps and four ten-foot poles to build a shelter for the van while painting. Other supplies included a paper jumpsuit, a breathing mask, and sealer for waterproofing.

While I was surfing the web for auto painting classes, I happened to click on a site that taught people how to yodel. I signed up then and there. Twenty-nine dollars and ninety-nine cents later I was a bona fide Yodelqueen. This was a perfect new skill to practice while I painted, although I left before my Certified Yodeler certificate arrived in the mail.

Once the materials were all gathered, the shelter erected, and the LandJet cleaned and primed, I thought it best to dig some more before starting on the van. Several days had passed since I'd last worked in the yard and it seemed rude to start painting when that huge piece of metal was still blocking the final posthole for Holly's garden fence.

So I dug and I dug and yodeled and yodeled, and when darkness came, I backed the LandJet out of its shelter and returned to the hardware store to buy a high-voltage construction lamp and a hundred-foot extension cord. I worked until three in the morning and slept in my clothes until daybreak. When I returned to the garden, Holly was there holding two mugs of green tea. A swath seven feet wide and fifteen feet long had been carved diagonally through the center of the garden. Holly handed me the tea and said, "I see you've been busy." Over the months we had become friends, and even though she was an unreformed criminal, it was clear having such a good memory worked both ways in that the bad things she did were just as easily recalled as how many aces were still in the deck.

I pointed at the length of metal running along the bottom of the channel I'd dug. The object was army green and a black boundary had been painted a foot inside the edges. Black square letters read: WALK INSIDE THE LINES. "It's a wing," I said. "It'll probably be too heavy for me to lift."

"There's someone I'd like you to meet." Holly said. "Someone who can help you."

"Do they have a backhoe?" I pointed at the wing again. "Because that's all we need to get this thing out of here."

"He's a doctor. A good one. He can't see you until Friday." She took a sip of her tea. "Can I call him back and confirm the appointment?"

It was Tuesday morning. Friday seemed like an eternity away, so I nodded and set to work painting the LandJet. The skies were clear with no wind to worry about blowing dust or knocking down my tarps, and by afternoon, I had one side of the vehicle finished. Your image dried overnight and the next day I matched the other side of the van and sprayed the stenciling along the auto's midsections. I let the sealer dry for a day and on Thursday night had a long dinner with Holly. She must have known about my plan to run the whole time we sat in her kitchen. She didn't press me to stay or even bring up the following day's psychiatrist's appointment. Instead we talked about movies and she told me her favorite places to travel.

Seattle was on my mind. The wing was a sign. Boeing was in Seattle and I was now convinced you were, too. When I crept the LandJet down the driveway later that night, Holly's silhouette stood in the distance watching me flee. She didn't wave and she didn't try to stop me. I mouthed the word "goodbye" and then rolled down the window and yodeled.

Lily's Baby

—⁘—

I feel like running away again. The chief and his lieutenants will be here in less than two hours wanting to know where Lily has hidden her secret films, and the truth is, I don't know. Last I saw, Lily was dropping the disk into her blue and white handbag yesterday afternoon in her apartment. Then we were apart for two hours while I went home to shower and change for the season finale party. She could have hidden the disk anywhere during that time. The cops will also want to know who is on the disk doing what, and I am not going to tell them. This is Lily's baby, not mine, and knowing Lily, she has a plan for its debut. I'm worried about her safety, but she knows where that disk is, and if she wanted to, she could surrender it right now.

When Officer Ryan's men arrive my job will be to say nothing, which would be easier if I could reach my purse and get my meds to knock me out for a bit. I don't normally rely on my drugs to hide, but today is different. I'm exhausted, my hand hurts, and I'm not sure about holding my own against four badgering policemen.

So I ring for a nurse hoping to see Boy-Soy again because I'm going to need his help, but a different guy arrives. He looks like he's from somewhere in South America and is thin, lithe, and cute in an androgynous way. His hair is spiked, full of gel, and bleached. He looks more like a backup dancer than a nurse. "You rang," he says with a theatrical flourish until he realizes the person in the hospital bed is me, which makes him gasp and cover his mouth with his hand.

"Did I scare you?" I ask him.

"You really are here! I thought the girls were playing mean jokes on me."

"Slow day at the nursing station?"

He puts both hands on his hips and replies, "They're nothing but witches and vipers down there."

I laugh and ask, "Which one are you?"

"I'm a good witch," he says.

"Maybe you can help then. See that cop out there?"

The nurse glances at Marcus. "I haven't taken my eyes off him since he got here."

"Not him...the other one. He's been acting like a jerk all morning."

"Should I get a doctor?"

"No, but do me a favor, when you leave the room send the cute one in, then walk about halfway down the hall and call for the other cop's help."

The nurse looks at me suspiciously. "What are you up to?"

I grin and say, "I promise I'm a good witch, too."

He pretends to be irritated and says, "That's my line," and stomps away.

Marcus enters the room and asks, "What's up?"

I point at the bag by the window and say, "In ten seconds that nurse is going to yell for help. When he does, hand me my purse then watch the door to make sure Officer Ryan is down the hall...please?"

Marcus doesn't look like he approves of what's happening, but when the nurse screams, he rushes to my bag and throws it from the windowsill to my lap as he speeds back to the doorway.

None of the contents in my bag are familiar. The lip-gloss is the wrong shade. The handle of my hairbrush has changed colors. The pink leather Kate Spade wallet Jack gave me has turned black and grown a Prada label. I open the wallet and find a New York State driver's license with Lily Durfee's picture. She's tan and smiling and her blue eyes are bright enough to pop through the lamination. The bag's inner pocket I designed to hide my pill organizer contains an unlabeled DVD in a clear plastic case.

"He's coming," Marcus says.

"How much can I trust you?" I ask him.

He looks me square in the eyes. "With your life."

I hand him the disk and he slides the case into his pocket while grabbing Lily's handbag and placing it back on the windowsill. If I've got Lily's bag then she's got mine, which means the kidnappers have pilfered my wallet and are probably on their way to get me. Fear not, last night was our season finale party and I knew I wouldn't need my phone, credit cards, or

ID, so the only things in my bag were my meds, a clean pair of underwear, and some flip-flops in case my heels started to bother me. The looks on the kidnappers' faces must have been priceless when they were rifling through my stuff. Lily has got to be loving me right now. All the pills probably freaked her out, and now she knows I'm sick, but at least her baby is safe.

"I gotta take my lunch break," Marcus says looking over his shoulder to the hallway. "You want another Gatorade?"

"Do you know what's on that disk?"

"What disk?" he replies, and with those two words I know I can trust him.

Miss Drumstick

W hen I slipped away from Holly's, Seattle was three thousand miles down the road, which translated into forty-eight hours of driving, and my goal was to be there in three days. As the sun came up I was heading north out of Florida on Interstate 75 and the sheer monotony of rest stop after rest stop and fast-food chain after fast-food chain began to spoil my momentum, so I decided to utilize the LandJet's GPS system and headed west from Macon, Georgia, finding myself in Eclectic, Alabama. The town was cluttered with signs announcing the next day's annual "Eclectic Fest," and I just had to stay for the night and see what the festival was all about.

It felt good to sleep in the LandJet again, which was surprising. Holly had given me one of the mannequins of you, so I wasn't lonely, and we stayed up most the night talking. I wanted to bring you to the festival the next day, but you were too heavy to carry around, so I left you sitting shotgun and even rolled down the windows a crack so you wouldn't get stifled.

"Eclectic Fest" didn't live up to its name. The event was your typical small-town fair, complete with cotton candy, ceramics booths, local musicians, and a chili contest. The oddest draw was the pregnant bikini pageant. Six women, all in their third trimester, posed onstage in skimpy two-piece bathing suits. An emcee asked them questions about the conception of the expected child. The contestant who told a story of hurried love in the meat locker of the supermarket where she and her boyfriend worked won and was titled "Missed Period."

The crowd was drunk on cheap beer and the sex stories were making the guys rowdy, so I snuck off towards the LandJet, followed by two men whose best features were their shoulder-length mullets. Just as I was approaching the van one of them called out, "Y'ain't from round here, ain't cha?"

I looked the men over. They were both wearing blue jean shorts and high-top sneakers with long white tube socks. One man had paint splattered all over his shorts; the other man's socks had grass stains around the ankles. "I'm from New York," I said.

The painter asked, "New York like New York City?"

The LandJet was just a few feet away. I was standing close to the driver's side door. The men stared at your painting on the side of the vehicle, and then the one with the grass stains said, "That's a hell of a paint job you got there."

I didn't reply, so the other man added, "Lookin' for yer sister, are ya?"

"Actually she's sitting in the front seat."

Grass Stains ran his hand down the shaggy mane of his mullet and said, "Well, it looks like we backed our asses into a double date then, didn't we Vern?" He looked at Vern and smiled.

"I like your hair," I told him.

He nodded a sincere thank you and replied, "It's called a Kentucky Waterfall."

Vern chimed in, "Business up front, party in the back," and turned his head to the side to not be outdone. He chugged the remains of the beer can he'd been carrying and pitched it underhand to the ground beside us. "Now," he continued, "about this here double date."

I reached in my shorts for the car keys and unlocked the doors with the remote. Without looking at the men, I climbed in the front seat and locked the doors. They circled around the front of the vehicle and saw you sitting beside me. Something scared them and they backed away. As I drove off, I heard one of them yell, "Freaky bitch!"

We tore out of Eclectic on Highway 78 heading northwest on a direct line towards Seattle, but then the urge to swim in the Mississippi river struck, so we veered off course and headed due west. We could have continued going north and staying on track because the Mississippi runs through Memphis, which wasn't even that far away, but Memphis is in Tennessee and I had to swim in the Mississippi River *in* Mississippi.

The AM radio kept us company as we hopped on Route 4 and passed through Wyatte, Senatobia, Sarah, and Dubbs. A religious show devoted two hours to discuss recent sightings of the Virgin Mary. The first sighting had been by a mother and daughter who'd found a pretzel twisted into the form of the holy figure. They received national attention for their discovery and eventually sold the pretzel to an Internet casino for fifty thousand dollars.

The second sighting had been a salt stain on the wall of an underpass in Chicago that vaguely resembled the droopy outline of a robed woman cradling a baby. Thousands of people from around the globe flocked to the site to burn candles, leave flowers, and write messages of peace. The radio host whispered that these sightings come in sets of three. He said all we could do now was pray and wait for the next incarnation of the Virgin Mary to arrive. The LandJet continued its trek westward and I patted your knee and wondered aloud how people could be so desperate.

Some time in the middle of the night we arrived at Mhoon Landing, Mississippi. The LandJet was docked at an RV campsite and I climbed into the cabin and slept through the entire next day all the way until the following sunrise. The van's interior smelled like stale fast food. You sat stoically in the passenger seat and didn't complain once.

We spent two more nights in Mhoon Landing at Fitzgerald's Casino and then hit the road again, crossing the great muddy waters on Highway 49 and heading due west through Arkansas, before swerving northward to hook up with Highway 67 and stop for the night in Pocahontas. We knew Pocahontas was our destination before leaving the Fitz because of all the advertising for the Annual Pocahontas Summer Dance. Returning to the road brought a fresh sense of freedom, and we were well rested and pampered after our stay at the casino. I didn't gamble once, but brought you to my room, and together we watched television and movies and ordered corn bread and catfish from room service.

That was the first time I saw Lily Durfee on TV. She was the star of a breath mint commercial in which she rode a bike through a sunny park filled with flowers and smiling people. I scanned the periphery of the screen for you in the background. The soundtrack played a song from the seventies. For the rest of the night I kept flipping through the channels trying to find that commercial again.

One commercial we couldn't avoid was the thirty-second spot for "the Party in Pocahontas," and even with all the buildup, I wasn't prepared for the madness the event would bring. The first morning of the PIP was the yo-yo convention. Hordes of yo-yo masters packed the fairgrounds performing Loop the Loops, Power Throws, Around the Corners, and Rock the Baby. A man wearing knickers, suspenders, and a rainbow-colored wig won the competition and a fight broke out when another contestant challenged the length of his string.

The Bubblefest followed. Bubble scientist Fan Yang was on site and I paid five dollars for him to enclose me in a single soap bubble. It was the safest I'd felt since we were kids and used to bury each other in pillows. The main attraction was when Fan tried to build a bubble wall one hundred and sixty feet long to break his record of one hundred and fifty-six feet, but the bubble burst when a spectator took a picture using a flash, which was something the audience had been instructed not to do before the show began. Fan was a gentleman, but he didn't try again, nor did he stay to sign autographs.

The night brought the Miss Drumsticks pageant, which involved women standing onstage hidden behind a curtain revealing only their legs to a panel of judges. Anyone could compete, so as a gag I entered and made the effort of carrying you with me. The man organizing the event was drunk and towing a chimpanzee that smoked cigarettes. When he realized I wanted to bring you onstage with the rest of the contestants, he liked the idea so much he waved our entry fee.

Neither of us thought you would win, Jamie, but you did, and when they raised the curtain and revealed the faces and bodies of all the competitors as well as the fact that the newly crowned Miss Drumstick was a mannequin, all hell broke loose. Boos and jeers were followed by half-eaten chicken legs flung at the stage. The crowd felt cheated and tricked, and as I watched the mob growing angry, the man with the smoking chimpanzee quietly made his was way towards a side exit.

All eyes focused on us, so I threw you over my shoulder and ran backstage, bursting outside through a fire exit, which set off a loud alarm. News stations from Memphis and Little Rock were covering the PIP, and two reporters chased me with cameras. When I made it to the LandJet I locked all the doors, closed the curtains, and curled beneath a blanket on the couch. A crowd circled around the vehicle and the shouting subsided to murmurs. Beneath your portrait was stenciled HAVE YOU SEEN MY SISTER? along with my cell phone number, and the sight usually stopped people in their tracks.

Someone knocked politely on the driver's side window, and when I looked from behind the curtain, all I could see was a bright light and the lens of a camera. "May I ask you a few questions about your sister?"

So I stepped out of the van and began to tell the citizens of Memphis and Little Rock your story, and by the time the interview was over, a tour of the LandJet had been given and you and your award-winning legs had been filmed sitting next to me on the couch. We must have looked like happy sisters except one of us was made of plastic.

American Idol

—⁓—

Since highway 67 brought us such good luck, we decided to follow the road north into Missouri and all the way to St. Louis. The man on the religious channel back in Mississippi had said miracles come in sets of threes, so when I saw the parking signs for the *American Idol* auditions, which is a pageant of sorts, I had to investigate further, having already attended the Pregnant Bikini and Miss Drumstick contests. Tryouts for the TV show didn't begin for two days and were to be held inside the Edward Jones Dome, where the NFL's St. Louis Rams play. The St. Louis Arch was visible from the stadium's parking lot, but the line of hopeful Idols snaking around three sides of the facility was even more breathtaking. The throngs of people frightened me, and since it was late at night, I decided to lie down on the couch in the back of the LandJet and get some sleep.

In the morning the line had gotten longer. It was the beginning of summer and the entire country had not received any rain for over two weeks, so the weather was perfect for standing in a line with five thousand lunatics. I debated walking around the stadium and checking out the scene, but something about all those people made me stay in the van. Eventually, I got hungry, so we drove into town.

In honor of the visiting *American Idol* auditions, a local barbecue joint named Thunder Hog was hosting its own competition: the Pig Olympics. Six piglets competed in running, hurdles, hoop jumping, and even diving and swimming for the title of "Swine Idol." The pigs competed once an hour and the same piglet was dubbed Swine Idol three times in a row. I hung around the restaurant a long time and justified my presence by continuing to order food. When the afternoon was nearing its end, I was covered in barbecue sauce and bean juice. Days had passed since my last shower, so I found a hotel and brought you up to the room so we could rest for the night and watch some television.

A long hot shower combined with an overstuffed stomach made me sleepy. The television was tuned to CNN and my consciousness drifted between dreams and the voice of the personality hosting the news show. The host had just finished giving a movie review and was leading into a segment called "Small Town, USA," and my eyes popped open at the words "Miss Drumstick."

I raised myself up on my elbows and saw the inside of the tiny theatre we'd visited in Pocahontas two nights before. When the shot moved in on the rising curtain and focused on you, I sat up completely. By the time the show was airing the footage of you and me sitting on the couch in the LandJet, I was standing two feet from the screen. When the segment ended, they cut to commercial, and there was Lily Durfee riding through the happy park, her breath as fresh as flowers.

I turned on my cell phone for the first time since the HSN shows and it immediately began to ring. The news had broadcast my number at my request for people to call with information on your whereabouts. The first call was a man asking if I was single. The second call was a woman claiming to have psychic powers. The third call was Mom, and I quickly hung up, turned the phone off, and climbed beneath the sheets.

In the morning I had eighty-one messages. Apparently, they had shown the Miss Drumstick segment every hour between 5:00 p.m. and 5:00 a.m. Jack sent a text saying we were all over the Internet. America couldn't get enough of the story about how a mannequin had won a beauty contest. People were more caught up in the humor of the situation than they were in the fact that you were missing. I checked us out of the hotel and headed back to the *American Idol* auditions, wondering what had happened to our nation's priorities.

When we arrived at the Edward Jones Dome, the parking lot was teeming with hopeful idols. I walked your mannequin to the end of the line and people recognized us and asked what we planned to sing. I didn't have an answer, but the line was so long, there was plenty of time to think. Then one of the *Idol* producers pulled us aside and walked us to the front of the line; traveling with the reigning Miss Drumstick had its privileges.

The host of *Idol* thanked us for coming and told us everyone affiliated with the show was pleased by our attendance. He interviewed us on camera, playing up the angle that you were missing and that I'd come to the audition hoping to find you or anyone who might know you. He knew Mom was the CEO of B-Global—they had mentioned it on CNN when showing the PIP coverage—and asked what she was doing to weather this family tragedy? He wrapped with the sentiment that many dreams can come true on *American Idol* and led us into the room with the judges. The cameras were rolling as I recapped our story again. Then they asked what I was going to sing.

I patted your head and told them you would perform. They looked at us strangely for an awkward few seconds until the British judge said, "Carry on, then."

So I turned to you and asked, "Ready?" After a pause, I said, "Here she goes." The room was completely still as I counted to twenty in my head. After the long period of silence, I said, "Thank you." The judges didn't know how to react, nor did the crew working the cameras and microphones. After more silence we left the room. They never even told us whether or not we were going to Hollywood.

On our way out of the dome, all the people who'd cheered us before the audition chose not to notice our departure and we boarded the LandJet and headed west on Interstate 70 averaging eighty-five miles an hour. Winds were high and the vehicle shimmied every time we passed an eighteen-wheeler. A hailstorm came so hard and fast, we had to pull over beneath an underpass and wait out the storm. I looked for a figure of the Virgin Mary on the wall, but only saw the spray-painted message, "Virgil is a frogboy." Within minutes the clouds passed and the sun shone brightly. Nothing had gotten wet. The pavement, the LandJet, even the grass divider between the two strips of highway, was dry. The whole experience reminded me of when a baby throws a tantrum in the final minutes before falling asleep.

By late afternoon we had crossed the state of Missouri and were heading north on Interstate 29 driving right along the border of Iowa and Nebraska, staying mostly within Iowa's boundaries except for a brief pass through Omaha. The rolling hills of Iowa were a sea of pastures and green fields, and traffic thinned with each northward mile. The space was relaxing and the sound of the wheels humming along the road was soothing. I reclined the driver's seat, loosened my grip on the steering wheel, and tuned into an AM station broadcasting from Wisner. The show was called *For the Birds,* and consisted of an hour of listener phone calls involving bird tales.

One man called from an airstrip in Wayne, where he'd bought a scream machine to keep crows off the runway. A farmer in Ponca painted his pigeons pink to ward off prey. The final call was from a woman in Plainview who was despondent because her favorite fowl, Lucky, had been snatched by a fox. Lucky picked her lottery numbers. The Powerball was fast approaching and she was sure she'd never win.

Sioux Falls, South Dakota, was only a few miles away, and soon we would have to switch roads and start heading west. I tuned out the radio and paid attention to the signs because I didn't want to miss our turn.

I exited Interstate 90 at the Ethan tollway. I was tired and didn't feel like talking to any person behind a counter, be it a gas station, restaurant, or hotel, so I parked the LandJet in the lot of a Wal-Mart, closed the curtains, and climbed into the back for some sleep. Ten minutes later there was a knock on the window. I ignored the call and waited for the visitor to go away. Soon I heard voices. A crowd gathered. They recognized the van from the news and the Internet. I turned on my cell phone and it immediately began to ring. Lights flashed outside the van. People were posing for pictures in front of your portrait. I was tired and wanted to be alone, and in time the moon rose higher and people sought their own shelter.

At four in the morning I peed in the parking lot and we vamoosed Ethan, cruising west until a town named Vivian caught my eye. The LandJet's GPS system indicated that heading north would lead us through the Fort Pierre National Grasslands and, eventually, into the Cheyenne River Indian Reservation. By the end of the day we had driven through both landmarks and arrived in a town named Mahto in the Standing Rock Indian Reservation. I found a dirt road and drove until it ended. We were surrounded by nothing but wilderness. I opened all the doors of the LandJet to let in some fresh air, and the silence was so deep, it was frightening. I turned the radio on for distraction, hoping to find a happy Top-40ish song, but everything on the dial was static. I hoisted you to the top of the LandJet and climbed up to join you. We lay on our backs looking up to the sky holding hands. The reservation grew dark and not one light flickered on the horizon, but the breeze above us was steady and strong.

The next morning Highway 212 took us out of the reservation and all the way across South Dakota. We had lunch near the state border in a town called Spearfish and then zipped through the northeast corner of Wyoming. It still had not rained and everything was covered with road grit and dust. I wiped your face with a T-shirt and promised to stop at a hotel in Montana.

We drove through Billings, then Bozeman, then Butte. By the time we reached Missoula the sun was beginning to rise again. We gassed up at Coeur D'Alene and cruised through to Washington. I'd driven twenty-four hours straight and didn't feel the least bit tired. Seattle was in our sights, and the sky was as blue as your bright morning eyes.

My eyes were growing weary. Driving through the night had made them bloodshot and dry. When we passed the sign for the Snoqualmie Falls campsite, a strange power steered the van through the gates of the Mount Baker-Snoqualmie National Forest, where we paid a fee and were assigned a specific spot to park. We wound along a road lined with towering pines. The land was carpeted with moss and dead pine needles. There was a softness to the terrain, and the cover of so many branches supplied a feeling of safety that rivaled Fan Yang's bubbles.

Seattle was less than an hour away. The campsite was empty and the sky was clear. Our little corner of the campground was shaded and I cracked the front windows of the van for air, closed the curtains, and locked the door. You lay on the floor next to the couch with your head resting on a pillow made from a rolled up sweatshirt. I cuddled up next to you. It had been a long trip from Florida, but I was grateful we had been able to spend so much quality time together.

The Chief

—◊—

Before I tell you about what happened the next morning in the campground and describe our brief stay in Seattle, which didn't even last an entire day, I need to take a break because a crowd has gathered outside my room. The three men at the door are shaking Officer Ryan's hand and clenching his shoulders like old acquaintances. Unfortunately, Marcus is still on his lunch break, so he can't help me. The police chief and his two detectives weren't supposed to be here for another hour. They're early, which isn't good, because I haven't gotten any meds from Dr. Mawji yet, so I won't be able to knock myself out for the interrogation like I'd been hoping.

Officer Ryan ushers in his friends. "There are some people here to ask you some questions, Miss Davis," he says in an unfamiliar friendly voice.

The three newcomers are handsome and athletic white men. They're wearing well-tailored suits, expensive shoes, and the two younger men both have tans. The older man, who must be the chief, has salt-and-pepper hair that looks professionally styled. The three of them seem more like politicians than policemen.

The oldest man sits in the chair next to me, while Officer Ryan and the other two stand in a row at the foot of my bed, blocking the door and the view of me from the hallway. The chief settles into his chair and removes a small notebook from the inside pocket of his blazer along with a silver pen. "This will only take a few minutes. Lily Durfee's whereabouts are still unknown and every hour she's missing makes finding her that much more difficult. We're putting together a list of suspects. This kidnapping is unusual because the ransom is a secret recording which we're not even sure exists?" He looks at me like he's waiting for an answer. I stare back blankly. After a moment he continues, "So the first thing you can do is tell us about these recordings."

Officer Ryan is trying to intimidate me with a menacing stare, so I decide not to speak and see how long it takes until the chief fills the silence. I pretend it's a game and count to seventeen.

"Miss Davis," the chief continues, "is it true that on Lily Durfee's apartment door there was a poster-sized disclaimer stating that the area was being filmed for commercial purposes?"

"Yes," I tell him. "You see them in Central Park all the time when they're filming commercials or—"

The chief cuts me off. "Well, here's the thing, we talked to your producers and they said they never filmed one scene in Lily's apartment, nor was it ever on the production schedule or even scouted as a possible location. The other odd thing is that every visitor to Miss Durfee's apartment had to sign a release that said they knew they were being filmed, and that these films belonged to *El-Dee Productions*."

"That's right," I say. "If you didn't sign the release, the doormen didn't let you upstairs."

"And it's our understanding that El-Dee Productions has nothing to do with your show, *Silly Little Rich Girl*." The chief is loosening and thinks he's getting somewhere.

"Exactly," I say, nodding enthusiastically. "El-Dee Productions is Lily's company, it has nothing to do with the network."

"Well, we've spoken to a couple of people who visited Lily's apartment and they were under the impression that the release they signed was for her television show, not some personal project of Miss Durfee's."

"Hmm," I take a moment to ponder. "Well, did they sign the release?"

"Yes," the chief says, "but . . ."

"The release was pretty specific," I say. "Who did you talk to?" Chief doesn't appreciate being interrupted. Officer Ryan continues to glower at me, so I keep playing dumb and blabber on, "I mean, have you seen the release? It's pretty obvious what it says." I smile at all four men, sweet as pie.

"Miss Davis," Chief says, with an edge beginning to creep into his voice, "have you seen any of the footage from these secret films?"

"What secret films?" I ask, sounding thoroughly confused.

The chief looks again at Officer Ryan. They're almost out of patience. "The films from the hidden cameras, Miss Davis. The films the kidnappers want."

"I'm confused. If everyone signed a release, then how are they secret?"

Chief glances quickly at Officer Ryan and then asks, "Just tell me this, Miss Davis, have you seen the footage?"

"You mean the television show? Of course, it was on TV." I point my thumb at Officer Ryan and add, "His daughter Layla loved it. You should talk to her, too."

Officer Ryan can no longer contain himself. "Stop playing with us and tell us what you saw!"

I look from the chief to Officer Ryan then back to the chief again, and say, "Fine, but I don't see why you have to get all huffy about it. It's mostly just me and Lily hanging out in our underwear. Lily liked to do that. The first thing she'd do when she got home was strip to her bra and panties. You know how some people make their guests take off their shoes before they enter their house? Well, Lily's rule was you had to strip down to your underwear before coming inside." I look at Officer Ryan and say, "Even you."

This was the secret of *Silly Little Rich Girl's* success: when people think you're stupid, they never catch on when you're acting stupid. This one simple truth was the entire foundation for a television show with no script, millions of viewers, industry-leading ad revenues, and a trail of victims left scratching their heads.

Officer Ryan yells, "That's enough! Do you want to help your friend or not?"

"But I don't even know who these men are," I reply. "None of them have even shown me a badge yet."

The chief puts his notebook and silver pen in his pocket. He didn't take one note. He watches me press the call button for a doctor and stands up. In a matter of seconds the room is empty except for Officer Ryan. He decides to unplug the TV as some sort of punishment, and Dr. Mawji arrives right as he pulls the cord from the wall.

"Officer Ryan was just unplugging my television set," I tell the doctor. "Can you plug it in for me once he leaves?"

Dr. Mawji doesn't know what to say. The power cord to the television lies limp beneath the electrical outlet at Officer Ryan's feet. "We need her to rest," Officer Ryan explains, "not watch TV."

Dr. Mawji marches to the wall socket and plugs the TV back in. "What we need is for you to do your job. Perhaps we should let the doctors be doctors and the police be police?"

The implied insult is not lost on Officer Ryan. He stares good and long at Dr. Mawji, who stares back equally defiant.

I interrupt the staring contest by saying, "Thanks for coming, Doctor. I buzzed you because I need my meds. In the morning I only take Lexapro and Lithium, but I'm feeling kinda anxious right now and some Klonopin would really help." I look at Officer Ryan and twirl my finger next to my temple to signal that I am crazy, humming the soundtrack from Lily's old breath mint commercial. In a few minutes the doctor will bring me my medicine, and once the Klonopin kicks in, everything will seem like a sunny-day bike ride through a flowery park where crooked cops and fake detectives don't exist.

Shirtless in Seattle

—◦◦◦—

Sunny days don't happen often in Seattle, but during the two weeks we spent driving from the southeast corner of the U.S. to the northwest corner of the country, the weather had been dry except for the brief pelting of hail we encountered in Missouri. By the time we reached the Mount Baker-Snoqualmie National Forest campground, the LandJet was caked with dust and the van's grille, headlights, and windshield were peppered with crushed insects. Five days had passed since my last shower and I was just as filthy as our vehicle.

When we laid down to rest, the campground was empty, but in the morning when we woke, the place was filled with VW busses, beat-up vans, pickups topped with campers, some ancient Volvo sedans, and two large school busses painted with peace signs, blue skies, and Mother Earths. The sun was just beginning to rise and already the area was teeming with people. Two campfires were burning. One was surrounded by men and women holding hands and chanting with their eyes closed, the other fire featured a bearded man playing the guitar to an audience of bobbing heads and marijuana smoke. The lot was strewn with beer cans, and it quickly became clear that these people were not waking up, but had never even been to sleep at all.

I slipped out the rear of the LandJet and peeked around the side of the vehicle towards the fires. The chanting had synched up with the strumming guitar and both groups were joined in a mantra growing louder with every beat. It seemed like the perfect opportunity to sneak across the grounds to the bathroom, but halfway there, someone spotted me and whistled loudly, halting both the chanting and my stride.

The bearded man put down his guitar and yelled, "You! Make yourself known!"

Panic went straight to my bladder and all I could do was wave and sprint to the bathroom.

Much time was spent washing my hands and face. I was stalling, using the shelter of the facilities to keep the bearded man away. The liquid soap was pink and dispensed from canisters above the sinks. It smelled like car wax and left a filmy residue on my skin. After three washes I left the bathroom feeling dirtier than when I had entered.

The fires had been extinguished and the two groups disbanded. The beer cans had been collected and the only sign of life was muted chatter seeping through the windows of one of the school buses. I walked cautiously toward the LandJet, spooked by the sudden desertion, and when I turned the corner of my vehicle to open the rear door, the bearded man was sitting on the van's bumper, idly whittling a stick with a large buck knife.

"What are you doing here?" he asked me.

"This is my van," I told him.

"Not here," he pointed around the campground with the blade of his knife and said, "*Here.*"

"I'm on my way to Seattle. I'm looking for my sister." I gestured toward your picture on the side of the vehicle.

He leaned around the corner of the van and looked at the portrait. "She's very pretty. So are you." He stood up and slid his knife into a sheath at his hips. "Do you know who we are?"

"Should I?"

"No." The tone of his voice was meant to scare me.

"If you don't mind," I said politely, "I really need to be on my way."

"We don't mind at all."

There were neither goodbyes nor handshakes, just me climbing into the front seat. I'd left the van unlocked and fortunately the keys were still under the floor mat. I quickly steered us out of the parking lot, too scared and too hurried to even check and make sure you were still lying peacefully on the floor of the cabin behind me.

It wasn't until I was floating above the waters of Lake Washington, riding a ferry from Mercer Island towards Seattle, that I realized you were gone. The bearded man or one of his minions must have stolen you from the back of the LandJet while I was in the bathroom. Nothing else was missing, only you. I walked to the railing of the boat, leaned over the edge, and stared at the water's whitecaps breaking against the ship's hull. A slew of gulls were following our path, swooping down to the vessel's deck to grab a tossed pretzel or a flyaway potato chip.

The Space Needle was visible in the distance, and I wondered if you were really walking the ground somewhere beneath its sphere, or if I was acting like one of those stupid sea gulls, trailing a path of discarded French fries and stale hotdog buns, plucking ceaselessly at an existence with negligible offerings and no tangible ending.

I didn't know what to do. I had now lost you twice, and after spending two weeks on the road with you, I suddenly felt very alone. The front seat seemed as big as the world. The center console was an ocean, the windshield a galaxy, and the passenger seat might as well have been on the other side of the globe. There was no place left on Earth that felt like home.

As the LandJet made its way closer to the city limits of Seattle, I couldn't bring myself to stop driving. I was filled with pessimism and disdain towards the entire American Northwest and its cultish mannequin-stealing citizens. So I kept heading west straight past the exits for Seattle's downtown. After eight blocks I ran out of land and reached the Puget Sound at the end of a road called Yesler Way.

There were signs for more ferries. One to Bainbridge Island, another to a place called Bremerton. This bothered me—all these cities starting with the letter B, and the only way to get there was by boat? How tedious and annoying. I couldn't imagine you ever wanting to live in a place where ferry schedules factored into your daily life.

This was all going through my head while I was stopped at a traffic light at the intersection of Yesler and Alaskan Way. A motorist behind me leaned on his horn, and I looked up at the traffic light and saw it change from green to yellow, then to red. I glanced in my rearview mirror and saw the man shaking his fist at me.

So I got out of the LandJet and marched towards him. His eyes and tiny hole of a mouth expanded with each step I took in his direction. He tried to smile, but I ignored the gesture and rapped on his window with my knuckles. He rolled the glass down and I leaned towards the opening and shouted, "What's the matter? Trying to catch a ferry?"

He was visibly frightened, this man who was fit, in his forties, dressed in khakis and a collared shirt, and driving a luxury sedan. I caught a glimpse of myself in his partially lowered window. My clothes were dingy and stained with soda, ketchup, donut glaze, and two weeks worth of grit. My hair was tangled and greasy. But more frightening than my appearance was the deranged look in my eyes, and I collapsed to my knees right there at the intersection of Yesler and Alaskan and began to weep at the unrecognizable person I had become.

Traffic was piling up and more people began to honk their horns with different pitches and durations. It was a chorus of ill will, a symphony of loathing, and the cacophony was all directed at me.

The scared man stayed in his fancy car and I pounded the side of his door screaming that I was sorry, screaming that I wasn't there to hurt him. A woman driving a station wagon who was stuck behind him got out of her car and picked me up off my knees. She walked me to the LandJet and noticed the stenciled message and your portrait and said, "I read about you on the Internet. Your sister isn't here, Angel. Trust me. I know these things."

I ripped my arm from her grasp, aimed my violent eyes into hers, and spat, "What do you know?"

She held the door to the van open while I climbed inside, and then she replied, "This afternoon the skies will open and it will rain harder than any rain you have ever experienced. Your life will be changed after the storm and you will become something more than you are now." She smiled then, shutting the door softly before leaving me with a knowing wink.

My hysteria vanished with that wink of her eye, and I slowly edged the LandJet towards Alaskan Way, making a right and heading north. A few moments later I turned left into a parking lot at Waterfront Park and found a bench to sit on, where I stared out across the Puget Sound and up towards a blue sky that showed neither clouds nor traces of rain.

Everything was wrong, Jamie. I had just driven three thousand miles and felt farther away from you than when I was back in the bungalow in St. Petersburg. There was an undeniable feeling that a mistake had been made. Mom's voice crept into my head telling me I was ridiculous, listing the sums of money wasted on gas and lodging, yelling at me to hurry up and get back to Wall Street.

But I didn't want to cry anymore, and I had no tears left in me anyway, so I turned towards the cityscape looming at my back and decided to walk through the streets of Seattle with an open mind, an open heart, and a set of open eyes, hoping that by the grace of a greater being I would find you.

I began walking eastward on Pike Street, and with each block, my spirits lifted. I decided to start over and reintroduce myself to Seattle. It had been a tough morning losing you, and the best way to remedy the situation was to get a Starbucks coffee and drink it on the observation deck of the Space Needle.

The elevator ride from the ground to the top of the needle takes only forty-one seconds, and soon I was walking the outer perimeter reading colorful signs that provided facts and graphics about the landmarks below. My favorite view was to the southwest, where I could look out over Puget Sound, the Olympic Mountain Range, and West Seattle Alki Point. A sign advertising the complimentary Swarovski telescopes bragged they were powerful enough to pick out a person sitting in the stands at nearby Safeco Field. As impressive as this might have been, I hadn't a clue which direction to aim the lenses to try and find you.

I panned the scope eastward and down towards the street and lost my breath when I saw the bearded man from the Snoqualmie campground conducting a rally with all his followers. The cult was gathered outside a McDonalds hoisting signs about rainforests in Brazil and U.S. capitalism. They were yelling at passersby and hurling squids from a catapult into the fast-food chain's storefront.

Then I saw you.

You had been changed out of your HSN costume and into McDonalds uniform pants and a hat, but they'd left your shirt off and written $LUT on your belly beneath a black bra very similar to the one Mom gave me. They had tied you to a cross that had been erected on top of one of their school busses, and drawn scars on your face and black rings around your eyes. The bearded man held a lighter to the cuffs of your uniform pants and set you ablaze.

Forty-one seconds wasn't fast enough to get me back to the ground. When I reached the sidewalk, my point of reference had changed and I no longer knew which way to run. I guessed, and guessed wrong, and by the time I found my way to the terrorized McDonalds, the group had already fled.

I stood across the street from the McDonalds watching a balding man with long sideburns mop up the dead squids that had splattered against the windows. Thunder cracked overhead and a gust of wind blew my sticky hair across my face. The drops of rain were large at first. Thunder cracked again and the drops fell with greater frequency and shrunk from dollops to beads. Again the thunder cracked, and the rain fell in curtains, thicker and heavier than the drapes they use on Broadway.

The temperature dropped fifteen degrees in a matter of minutes, but I didn't care. I was soaking wet and it was the first shower I had taken in almost a week. When my clothes got heavy, I took them off. I'd been wearing the black one-piece bathing suit as underwear, and walked the eight blocks back to Waterfront Park in a slow gait. This would be my first and last day in Seattle, and I vowed to never return to this Godforsaken city again.

The Virgin Mary

I arrived back at the parking lot soaking wet in my bathing suit, only to find a crowd gathered around the LandJet. The people were not fazed by the rain or the thunder or the wind, and when lightning crashed into the waters of Puget Sound, not one person looked away from the van to notice. They were all staring at the portrait of you. The image had changed. The furious rain had made the paint run, and now there was a mass of people surrounding your ruined image holding hands and saying prayers. I pretended the van wasn't mine and looked odd standing in the pouring rain wearing nothing but a bathing suit, carrying my wallet and car keys, but no one looked at me twice.

"What's everyone staring at?" I asked an elderly lady. She was Hispanic and wearing a scarf over her head. In her hands she clutched several plastic grocery bags that were filled mostly with produce and fruit.

She pointed at where your portrait used to be and said, "It's the Virgin Mary."

I eased away from the crowd never turning my back on them. The rain was still pouring down, but the paint on the van had stopped running, and it really did look like the silhouette of a woman shrouded in robes cradling an infant swathed in a blanket. I thought of the radio announcer back in Arkansas who'd said miracles come in sets of three. In the corner of the parking lot was a sign for the ferries heading towards Bainbridge Island and Bremerton, and for some reason, my thoughts jumped to Boulder. It would be the third place I looked for you, and I had nothing left but to believe a miracle would be there waiting.

Obviously I needed the van. The crowd was growing and a tourist with a video camera was filming the action. I snuck three rows of cars away and crouched behind a silver pickup with tinted windows so that I could watch without being sighted. The only way to get in the van without having to face the crowd was to try and scare them away, so I ducked a little lower and pressed the unlock button on the LandJet's remote locking system.

The vehicle emitted a loud beep, the brake lights flashed, and the head-lights illuminated. Cameras began to shutter, "Hail Mary"s were uttered, and the Hispanic woman was so stunned, she dropped her bags of gro-ceries and a mango rolled under the carriage of the van. I pressed the Lock button again and the lights flashed and the alarm system beeped. The tourist with the video camera panned the lot, but I was hidden well. I unlocked and locked the vehicle a few more times, quickening the in-tervals of lights and alarm warnings.

The crowd did not disperse. If anything, their curiosity increased, but they did back away enough so there was room to make a dash through their circle to the front door. So I went for it and managed to lock myself in the van without too much conflict, although I did bang my shin on the vehicle's running board.

When I started the engine people were shouting for me not to leave. Two women hopped on the rear bumper and the tourist with the video recorder placed himself directly in the van's path. I leaned on the horn and slowly rolled towards him. We were engaged in a game of chicken and he held his ground until the hood of the LandJet was only inches from his camera.

People began running after the van waving their arms frantically and begging for me to stop. I made a right turn back on to Alaskan Way and the GPS monitor told me I was heading south. The gas tank was nearly full, and I punched Boulder, CO, into the GPS's keypad and waited for direc-tions. I was so intent on finding my way, I didn't even notice the line of cars that had begun to follow me.

The fastest route out of town was to get back on Interstate 90 and head east, which meant passing Snoqualmie Falls before turning south on In-terstate 82. I thought about going back to the campground and hunting down the bearded man and his followers, but then I noticed a convoy of news vans speed into the sights of my rearview mirror and realized that a massive troop of cars were bunched together, patiently trailing the Land-Jet. A burgundy minivan pulled alongside me, and a woman in her fifties riding in the passenger seat waved her cell phone, then held her hand to her ear in the universal "call me" sign. She watched me flip open my phone and it immediately began to ring.

"Hello?" I answered.

A panicked female voice asked, "Is this the woman driving the van?"

I instantly regretted using a different paint for my phone number. Your image morphed into the Virgin Mary, but the number remained unblemished. The whole situation almost made me laugh. "Leave me alone," I said into the phone.

"I can't believe I got through." She waved to me from her car. "We've been calling nonstop."

"Do you have information on the whereabouts of my sister?"

There was a pause before she said, "No."

"Do me a favor and roll down your back window."

Their back window lowered and I rolled down mine and slowed so that the openings lined up, then chucked my cell phone into her back seat and watched her pull over to the shoulder of the highway as I sped off towards the setting sun.

The convoy followed me through Selah, Union Gap, Sunnyside, and Umatilla. By the time I crossed the state line into Oregon, the van was running on empty, so I stopped to gas up in Echo. The crowd that had been following me for the past two hundred and fifty miles pulled into the truck stop behind me, quickly occupying every pump and filling the ample parking lot. The overflow of cars pulled around the side of the rest stop to the lot reserved for eighteen-wheelers, and soon that was full as well.

There was only one attendant on duty to pump everyone's gas and he was instantly overwhelmed. I hopped out of the van and expected a crowd to gather but no one bothered me. The people were gassing up, getting food, or just waiting for me to hit the road again. A few took pictures, but only from a distance, and I felt like an animal being tracked on safari. I was still dressed only in my black one-piece bathing suit, which made me feel even more self-conscious.

I was hungry and thirsty and when no one made a move to try and speak to me, I decided it was safe to run into the mart. I grabbed three bottles of water, a six-pack of Diet Coke, and a large bag of pretzels. The cashier was baffled and our exchange was awkward. Through his window he had a clear view of the side of the LandJet with the supposed Virgin Mary figure. He obviously didn't recognize the likeness and asked, "Are all you people traveling together?"

"I'm alone," I told him. "The rest of them are a group." He nodded and pinched the goatee growing on his chin.

On the shelves beneath the counter, someone had placed a magazine backwards and upside down, and the page facing outward was an advertisement picturing a blown-up image of an expensive watch doctored to look like a pool. The space inside the watchband was filled with water accentuated by a blonde woman in a white bikini serenely floating on a yellow raft.

I looked out the window at all the people waiting, and realized that ever since I'd left St. Petersburg, I'd mostly been surrounded by crowds. The pageants, the *American Idol* audition, the parking lot in Wal-Mart—even when I'd tried to rest in a remote campground, a group of people was there when I awoke. I looked again at the pool in the watchband and there was no place on Earth where I would have rather been. So I bought the magazine and ripped the back cover off, leaving the rest of the publication on the counter. It wasn't until I was walking back towards the LandJet that I looked at the ad again and realized the woman floating in the pool was Lily Durfee.

Then I was interrupted. "Want your phone back?" The woman from the burgundy minivan stood an arm's length from me with my phone in the palm of her hand.

I looked at the picture of Lily again. She looked comfortable and tan and well rested and fed. I suddenly felt frumpy in my black one-piece Speedo.

"Miss?" the woman asked me. "Your phone?" She was overweight, wearing jeans with an elastic waistband and a long-sleeved T-shirt branded with a smiley face and the message *Life is good.*

"I'm sorry," I told her. "But can't you people just leave me alone? And I don't mean that in a rude way, either."

"It isn't you we're interested in. It's the van...the Virgin Mary."

I took back my cell phone and tossed it in a bucket filled with sudsy water and a squeegee.

"Why are you such a skeptic?" she asked.

I pointed at the ruined image of you and said, "That used to be my sister. This is the second time she's been taken from me today, and that's no miracle."

"But it is," she argued.

"I just want her back," I said.

A calm smile grew on her face, and then she said, "Seek, and you shall find."

I looked at the picture of Lily floating in the waters of the expensive watch. She was lying on her back with her legs crossed at her ankles and her hands joined to make a pillow behind her head. I lay down on the black tar of the parking lot and mimicked her pose repeating the words "seek, and you shall find" over and over and over again.

After the brief pit stop the flock of Virgin Mary enthusiasts trailing the LandJet continued to grow. It had now been eight hours and several hundred miles since the paint of your portrait had streaked into this new entity, both dials up and down the radio gave updates on the LandJet's whereabouts, and some TV vans had joined the party. The nation's curiosity had been piqued, and soon enough folks came out to watch those watching the van. A botched paint job had set off an avalanche of curiosity, zeal, and blind faith.

When I arrived in Bliss, Idaho, midnight had already passed. The town was quiet and most of the storefronts on Main Street were unlit. I wanted to stop driving and rest, but felt safer being on the move. The LandJet was a cocoon, and as long as I kept driving, no one could speak to me. Near the end of the main strip, one building was lit and both sides of the street were lined with parked cars. I needed to stretch my legs and use a bathroom, and the one open establishment in town was the Bliss Bar.

I double-parked, locked the van, and ran inside. The lights were on and last call had been announced, but the twenty patrons chatted away unrushed, and not one head turned to notice me dash to the ladies' room in my bathing suit. The bathroom was only big enough to accommodate one person, and I leaned my back into the locked door and slid to the floor and collapsed.

When I unlocked the door and reemerged into the bar everything had changed. Twenty people had turned into two hundred, and several camera crews and reporters were panning the Bliss Bar interviewing anyone willing to talk. The lights had been dimmed and the jukebox was louder; last call and local ordinances had been shrugged off due to the arrival of the Virgin Mary.

I stood with my back pressed to the wall and hid behind a pay phone waiting for the right moment to sneak through the crowd. Within seconds I was spotted and enclosed by a semicircle of bright lights and shoulder-mounted video cameras. I quickly turned around and relocked myself in the bathroom. Reporters shouted questions from the other side of the door, notes were slid through the crack, and eventually the police arrived. They threatened to tow the LandJet because it was double-parked and unregistered. I opened the door a crack and looked into the steel blue eyes of a middle-aged mustached policeman who was barrel-chested and had a blond flattop as crisp and shiny as his badge. "Can you get me out of here?" I pleaded with him.

"That's what we been trying to do for the past hour, miss." A camera light shone over his shoulder and he swatted blindly behind him.

"Will you take me to your jail and give me my own cell? Seriously, I'll pay you if I can have a cot and some privacy."

He leaned into the crack of the door and asked in a softer voice, "You want me to lock you up?"

"Just cuff me and drive me away. Please? I promise I'll leave in the morning."

He looked over his shoulder at the circus of media and fanatics and his mouth curved into a frown. He instructed me to stick my wrists forward, then gently shackled on the handcuffs. "How about I drape my jacket over your head before I lead you out of here?" He spoke in a kind voice that let me know he was on my side.

I ducked and was soon covered in a body-warmed darkness tinted with the smell of deodorant. It was hard not to trip. All I could see was a thick forest of legs. I was headed towards the clink under the spotlight of several national TV cameras. My thoughts turned to Mom and what she must think seeing her daughter being dragged out of a bar in Idaho, wearing nothing but a bathing suit and handcuffs on national television. Blackberries belonging to the staff of B-Global's PR department would be ringing throughout the city. I thought it ironic that people were seeing the Virgin Mary on the side of a van once owned by a man who made women dress up as Minnie Mouse for his own perverted pleasure, but then again, the Lord does work in mysterious ways.

The next morning I had a visitor. A handsome man in his midthirties dressed in a suit and brown shoes humbly approached my cell and sat on a stool on the other side of the bars. He introduced himself as Chip

Coolidge and made a point of telling me he was happily married and already the father of four. He'd seen me on the news and had driven two hundred and fifty miles through the early morning hours just so he could be the first to talk to me. He even brought me some clothes—sweatpants and a T-shirt from Brigham Young University—which were a welcome change from the orange jumpsuit the Bliss County Jail had provided.

Chip's father had died a year earlier and left him a handful of the largest and most profitable car dealerships in Salt Lake City. Along with the businesses, Chip had also inherited his father's deep-rooted faith in Christianity, and he had driven the three and a half hours through the night to see me about buying the LandJet. He showed me a check for fifty thousand dollars.

I was feeling cagey. The night's rest behind bars had been pleasant enough, but I was still in a cell, and even though I was free to leave at any time, I was trapped by the fact that no matter where I tried to run, wherever I took the LandJet, people would follow. And then there was Chip Coolidge, full of faith, with his four healthy kids and his father's dealerships. "The vehicle is a LandJet," I informed him. "Are you familiar with those? It's only been driven five thousand miles and it is in mint condition."

"A LandJet," he repeated with a hint of regret in his voice. "The news didn't say anything about a LandJet. They just said it was a van."

"Oh, but Chip, it's so much more. The attention to detail in the interior rivals that of a masterpiece painting."

"I'm really only interested in the exterior of the van," Chip said, offering an optimistic smile.

"Well," I replied, "I can't really sell one without the other."

Chip shook his head and his smile faded. "See, what I want is to tour the van to all my different lots, maybe rent it out for weddings or other special events."

"Two hundred and fifty thousand," I declared.

"Dollars?" he asked, astounded.

I shrugged and said, "A chaplain in Chagrin Falls already offered me one fifty."

"A chaplain?" he asked skeptically.

Then I added, "You have no idea what I went through to get this van."

We settled on one hundred and fifty thousand dollars and a new, silver Toyota Prius from one of his dealerships. He agreed to drive me to Salt

Lake City and come back the next day for the LandJet, so we snuck out of Bliss, leaving the crowd of van worshippers praying by the chainlink fence of the pound. A few hours later, I was outfitted with a fat check and a shiny silver Prius from Chip's flagship lot in Salt Lake City, and on the road again.

Driving east on Interstate 70 with no baggage, a fresh odometer, and that new car smell made me feel like a different person. I still hadn't showered since the night before the *American Idol* audition, so after crossing the state line of Utah into Colorado, I checked into a Holiday Inn in Grand Junction. Four months had passed since leaving Manhattan and some time was needed to reflect on where I'd been and where I was going. Ever since Mr. Pervy's hotel room, strange events were either happening to or around me, and it wasn't clear if I was seeking these situations or if they were somehow following me.

I spent seven nights in the hotel, sleeping and watching the news. The media was still paying a lot of attention to the Virgin Mary sighting on the van. Footage of your mannequin burning at the cross above McDonalds surfaced, and once the connection was made that the mock crucifixion had occurred around the same time of your portrait's transformation into the Virgin Mary, skeptics became believers, believers became fanatics, and conspiracies floated that it had all been staged. Mom and B-Global were mentioned in every report, and after a few days she was asked to resign. She fought the board, but eventually the shareholders voted and she was given her golden parachute and Andrew was given his.

I had checked into the hotel under a fake name, paid cash for the room, and was driving a new car with temporary plates, so I could not be found. All I wanted was to forget about Seattle and start over. The talking heads on the TV set were calling for me, and I wasn't sure whether this was really happening, or if I was hearing voices in my head. I should have picked the phone up and called Mom for help, but she had lost her boyfriend and her job because of me, so I thought if I just kept looking for you, if I just kept running, eventually, things would work themselves out.

A Prayer for Misty and Memphis

———w———

D r. Mawji is in the hallway holding a small tray topped with little paper cups filled with my meds. Officer Ryan must have made a snide comment, because Dr. Mawji is scolding him with a pointed finger. When he walks into my room, he's shaking his head and places the tray on my bedside table. He refers to each container of pills as he speaks, "Here's your Lithium, your Lexapro, and I've brought you three doses of Klonopin, two at five milligrams and one at ten. You know better than me what you can handle, but I suggest starting with five. You've had a long night and a long morning, so five should probably be enough to get you sleeping." He looks at Officer Ryan in the doorway and adds, "But I brought you a little more in case you need it."

You should understand how much medication I take, Jamie, and why. One out of every five persons with bipolar disorder kills themselves, and usually it happens when they stop taking their meds. I should have been taking these pills the entire time I was on the road looking for you. I was just as sick then as I am now. I don't like these pills, though. I have to carry them with me everywhere I go, and every time I hear them rattle in my purse, I'm reminded that I'm sick and that I'm different and that at any time my mania could hit and split the earth right under my feet.

Marcus is back, Gatorade in hand. He shuts my door softly and walks over to the bedside table placing the drink next to the small paper cups with the meds. He's too polite to ask what they are. He pats his pocket where he's hiding the disk. "I don't think I can hold on to this much longer."

"You're right," I say. "I'm sorry. I should have never given it to you in the first place."

"It's a weird day today." Marcus looks around the room. "Something's off. Isn't it? Or do I sound like a crazy person?"

"You don't sound crazy at all."

"Chief'll be here in half an hour, maybe that'll help."

Trying to sound conversational, I ask, "Hey, what's he look like?"

"He's a tall, bald black man. Don't worry, you'll know who he is the second you see him." Marcus stops himself short and says, "Why do you ask?"

I swallow my Lithium and Lexapro and wash them down with a sip of Gatorade. Then I look at him and say, "Mmm, thanks again for the drink."

"Bullshit," he says. "Answer the question."

"I dunno, I was curious, Marcus. Jeez."

"So let me get this straight—I risk my job for you and you still won't tell me the truth?" He shakes his head. "You girls really are all the same, aren't you?"

"Yeah, we're all exactly one hundred percent identical. Just give me the disk back, okay? You guys are all the same."

"Who's all the same? Black people?"

I look him dead in the eyes and say, "Oh, please." I turn my head from him and stick out my arm, "Give me the disk and leave me alone."

"I'll give you the disk back once you tell me what's going on."

"That's blackmail."

He's grinning and there's a twinkle in his eye. He shakes his head and replies, "Not blackmail...police work."

I interpret his joke as a peace offering, so I reciprocate. "The chief was already here but he wasn't a tall, bald black man. Actually, I'm pretty sure it wasn't the chief at all, but that's who Officer Ryan said he was." Marcus looks into the hall at Officer Ryan and is about to call for him, but I quickly say, "Wait!"

"What's he holding over your head?"

"He overheard my medication: Lithium, Remeron, Lunesta, Zyprexa, Lexapro, Seroquel. They're antipsychotics and antidepressants and I don't really go around advertising that I'm on these pills because it tends to change people's perception of me, but your partner out there says he's going to tell the media unless I do what he wants." Marcus' expression suggests he doesn't understand why I would care, so to help explain, I say, "Nutbar, nutcase, loon, psycho, crackpot, screwball, weirdo, fruitcake, crackbrain, sicko, and as you like to say, crazy person."

He frowns because he didn't mean to hurt my feelings earlier, and then he says, "Kingfish, buckwheat, lawn jockey, banjo lips, jungle bunny, muffin head, moon cricket, coon, spade, nigger." He slaps his knee to punctuate the end of his inventory.

"So I take it you understand?" We're both smiling now and I say, "You left one out," as a joke.

Marcus laughs even harder and says, "One? Try a hundred!" He slips his hand in his pocket and says, "Was Officer Ryan really in here with someone who said he was the chief?"

"He was with three men. They definitely pretended to be cops." My mouth has gone dry, so I take a big sip of the Gatorade and then dump all three Klonopin into the bottle and watch them dissolve. "Give me the disk back, Marcus. I don't want to get you fired."

"I want to help you," he tells me.

I grab his hand and reply, "You already have."

Marcus slips me the disk, and it's quickly hidden between the mattress and my thigh, but it appears as if we're caught, because Officer Ryan rushes into the room hanging up his cell phone. He turns the television to Channel 5, and it's a huge relief he's not diving under the sheets to snatch the disk.

The TV screen is a split image shared by the faces of Misty and Memphis, the two strippers Lily had hired to waitress on the night of the poker game with the mayor's daughters. Earlier this morning, not long after Lily's kidnapping, Misty and Memphis were gunned down as they left their place of employment. The shooters were driving a black GMC Suburban, and because of the proximity in time to Lily's kidnapping along with the similarity of the vehicle used in both crimes, it is believed the two incidents are somehow connected.

I grab the bottle of Gatorade and swallow several big gulps. Marcus is watching and I can't look him in the eyes.

Officer Ryan paces to the foot of the bed and takes a defiant pose. "Well? Did you knows those girls or not?"

94

The Klonopin-laced Gatorade can't go down fast enough. Once every drop has been swallowed, I recline into the pillows, shut my eyes, and say, "Tell the chief I say hello."

A quick glance at Marcus confirms he's smiling. This makes it easier. The medicine will take a few minutes to do its work, but I can be patient. In the meantime, I will say a prayer for Misty and for Memphis, for Marcus and for Mom, and finally, I will say a prayer for the mayor's daughters, who know not what they've done.

Lily Durfee's Arrival

—⁓—

When I arrived in Boulder in my new silver hybrid and one hundred and fifty thousand dollars richer, I had been given a second chance to start my search for you. To go along with my new car, new riches, and new resolve, I got a new haircut as short as a boy's to celebrate the new me. The second course of action was to rent an apartment, and luck found me a two-bedroom unit with a balcony that overlooked Pearl Street, the main drag in town. When I wasn't working or out and about looking for you, I sat on my balcony above Boulder's busiest street with a pair of Nikon-7 15X35 action zoom binoculars hanging around my neck, ready to focus on any figure resembling yours.

I rented a two-bedroom apartment so I could sleep in one room and set up the second room as a headquarters. I bought an aerial map of the city and had it blown up into an eight-by-ten-foot rectangle, which I plastered to the wall and divided into sections with a grid, each box covering one square mile. Every day a different sector was canvassed and X'd out. Also in HQ were two large tables placed together to form an L-shaped desk covered with a laptop, telephone, police scanner, and a large desktop calendar on which I kept detailed notes regarding which quadrant of Boulder had been visited on what day. I also blew up the picture of you standing in front of the reservoir in Central Park and hung it on the wall to remind me of what you looked like.

This may sound silly, but in all my hyper-organization, I was growing more and more forgetful. I'd lock my keys in my apartment or forget where I parked my car. Sometimes, I'd walk out of my building onto Pearl Street and stop cold in my tracks not remembering where I was heading.

The other room was decorated exactly like the bedroom we shared when we were children: two twin beds, Winnie-the-Pooh sheets, and walls painted pink with baby blue trim. I even bought a bookcase and stocked it with our favorite bedtime stories. Sometimes at night when I couldn't sleep, I'd stay up for hours reading Nancy Drew aloud to the empty twin bed next to me.

The apartment had a kitchen/living area which I filled with bean bags, a large dollhouse, and fresh flowers bought every other day. I stocked the fridge with root beer and Swiss cheese, and filled the freezer with Tater Tots. These were your favorite things, and I thought if I built it, you might come.

The third part of my strategy was to find a job in a busy coffee shop and work as many hours as possible behind the counter toasting bagels and frothing milk while waiting for you to enter the café. Fortunately, my colleagues had no problem taking time off and asking me to cover their shifts. It seemed like every day either a band was in town or ski conditions were perfect; sometimes just the sun being out was enough of a reason for Boulderites to take the day off. Oftentimes I would work sixty, even seventy hours a week.

About a month into the job we were getting ready to close for the day, when I was overtaken by the urge to phone home. It was a Saturday afternoon and the place was empty, and for some reason, I just really needed to feel like I still had a family. Jack answered on the second ring, and the instant I heard his voice, my eyes filled up with tears and I realized just how much I missed him. The first few minutes of our conversation went well. It was strange to hear a familiar voice, a sibling's voice, and it made me want to untie my apron, hop over the counter, and run to the airport to fly home.

"Dude, you're like a celebrity," Jack said. "I'm gonna start selling your stuff on eBay if you don't get back here."

"Maybe you can come to Boulder and visit sometime," I told him. "You could help me look for Jamie."

He didn't like this suggestion. "You're not gonna find her, Liza. Jamie's dead. She has to be."

"Why would you say something like that, Jack?" It hurt to hear him speak these words and my voice almost cracked.

"Liza, where else could she be? Mom hired the best private detectives in Manhattan and they found nothing, and you've been all over the news trying to find her." He spoke calmly and sounded so grown up. I'd only been gone six months, and I marveled at how much a person can change in only half a year. "If she is alive," he continued, "there isn't a person in the country who doesn't know what she looks like and that her sister is looking for her."

"Well, maybe she's not in the country."

"Then stop looking for her in Colorado and come home."

Then Mom grabbed the phone from him and said, "He's right, Liza. You need to come home."

The sound of Mom's voice suddenly made me feel about two feet tall. We hadn't talked since our fight about Mr. Pervy and I was ready for the fireworks to start up again, especially since she'd lost her job after the Virgin Mary thing.

"I'm worried about you, Liza," she said with no bitterness.

"I'm sorry I got you fired."

"Don't be, it's the best thing that's ever happened to me."

"Are you still mad about Mr. Purdy?"

"No, honey. Didn't you get my messages?"

"What messages?"

"On your cell phone? I called you every day for two weeks straight." She started to sound annoyed. "You didn't get any of those messages?"

"I kinda had to throw my phone out," I said. "We won a beauty pageant and got on CNN, and after that too many people were calling."

"Who's 'we'?" Mom quickly asked.

"Me and Jamie," I told her.

"Jamie is gone, Liza. She's gone. As hard as that may be to accept."

I glanced at my coworker, Kem. She was a part-time yoga instructor, part-time barista. She wore her hair in a bandanna and didn't own a bra. Kem was wiping tables and throwing away used napkins. KBCO was playing a Keb' Mo' song, and she danced as she cleaned. The song on the radio changed to an instrumental with an Eastern Indian influence. Kem pressed her thumbs against her middle fingers and waved her arms at her sides like a snake charmer. She smiled at me as she moved her hips in time with the music.

"I think I have to go now, Mom." I hung up the phone and slipped underneath the counter to join Kem in her dance. We were the only people in the shop, and she wiggled closer and closer until we were only a few inches apart. Kem closed her eyes. We were moving together and I could feel the warmth of her skin. The mood in the room felt as if anything could happen.

From that afternoon on, Kem and I became friends and began a strange relationship that consisted of her inviting me over when her boyfriend was out of town. She always had a freshly rolled joint, which she would light on my arrival, and we'd pull all the pillows and the comforter off her bed and build a nest on her living room floor from which we would watch a movie or late-night TV. She often fell asleep within thirty minutes of my arrival. That was mostly her intention when inviting me over, to have a warm body to sleep next to. I accepted the invitation for the same reason. Lying next to Kem reminded me of when you and I would sometimes share a bed.

One night when Kem and I were buried beneath the blankets on her floor, Lily Durfee appeared on David Letterman. I didn't know Lily was going to be on and made no mention of knowing her, but Kem was only half awake and not paying attention, anyway. Lily's career had exploded after she got a gig modeling lingerie at Manhattan's Fashion Week. A picture was taken of her strutting down the runway in a pink set of panties and bra made from lace so fine and transparent, the dark circles of Lily's nipples and the thin strip of pubic hair beneath her waist were clearly visible. The Internet site Yahoo! decided to use this image as their lead photo for all their headlines about Fashion Week, and within hours, this picture became the most emailed photograph from their network. Lily held this title for eleven straight days and parlayed it into an appearance on David Letterman, promoting the lingerie by reading his Top Ten list in a silky light blue camisole above a stretchy pair of blue and yellow polka-dotted hipsters. The ratings were so high that night, she was asked back the following week to read another list, but Lily turned down the offer and convinced the producers to let her appear in a different role.

When Lily's second appearance aired, I was watching from the floor of Kem's apartment with Kem affectionately spooned against my back. In her bit, which she created herself, Lily went to Giants Stadium and interviewed the professional football players as they boarded the team bus en route to an away game. Most of the players were dressed in elaborate suits and they all carried briefcases. Lily picked the men wearing the most flamboyant clothing and asked if they'd be willing to show her what was in their totes. The premise being that these men were going to play football, why did they need to dress up, and what does one carry in a briefcase to a professional football game, anyway?

The football players ate out of her hand. Some of them had seen her lingerie shots on the Internet and commented, which she effortlessly spun into a joke. Most of the athletes knew Lily was making fun of them for carrying around sports car brochures and pocket Nintendo games in briefcases and business suits, but she handled the situation in such an affable manner, no one felt insulted. At the end of the clip the studio audience's applause continued for such a lengthy period, they cut to commercial before the clapping was finished. I turned off the TV set and nestled deeper into Kem's embrace, knowing that was not the last I would see of Lily Durfee. I was lost in thought and said aloud, "That was funny, wasn't it, Jamie?"

Kem stirred but didn't answer, which was good, because her voice sounds nothing like yours.

A few weeks later I invited Kem over to see the apartment. I'm not sure what freaked her out more: HQ with the aerial map, police scanner, and blown-up picture of you, or the twin beds, children's books, and the doll house. What really spooked her though, was when I showed her our bedroom and said, "And this is mine and my sister's room."

I wasn't trying to be weird, but the look in Kem's eyes made it clear I needn't bother to try and explain myself. She was leaving and she wasn't coming back. Ironically, that night I could have really used a friend. I stayed up until four in the morning listening to the police scanner. A peeping tom had been reported on Lee Hill Drive and a couch had been set on fire on the lawn of a fraternity. Other than that, not much else was going on.

Bruce

—⚡—

Following my conversation with Mom and Jack, I got more and more homesick and even began to doubt my theory regarding your location. With this uncertainty came the nursery rhyme chorus, so I bought another sewing machine to keep it at bay by designing some purses. Feeling rich from the Virgin Mary money, I splurged on the materials and bought calf leather, silk for lining, and sterling silver for buttons and snaps. I also had a local silversmith make an LD latch from a design I drew in my sleep. I don't even remember making the original drawing; I just woke up one morning and there it was scrawled on the pad of paper I left on my bedside table. This very design became my company logo and now you can find it in stores in twenty-seven different countries. But back in Boulder I never predicted such luck and achievement; in fact, I was mostly filled with despair after Kem ditched me, and I almost gave up looking for you altogether. A boy named Bruce kept the search for you alive, and if not for him, I would have never made it to Staten Island, and if I had never made it to Staten Island, I would have never gotten to where I am today. So in that roundabout way, I pretty much owe all my success to Bruce, which makes me feel even worse when I think about what I did to him.

Bruce would come to the coffee shop every Thursday and stay for hours, either hovering over a book or drawing elaborate sketches that he'd shield with his entire body as soon as anyone approached his table. He was by far our oddest customer, and I was immediately drawn to him. The first time we spoke was on Thanksgiving as I was closing the coffee shop early. Bruce had been sitting at a table in the back corner all morning and was the only customer remaining. I was sweeping the floor and placing chairs upside down on tabletops, a surefire way to clear any lingering coffee drinkers, but Bruce hardly noticed. The music's volume was muted, and the dominant sounds in the building were the bristles of my broom brushing the floor accompanied by the percussion of dishes being stacked in the kitchen.

The past few hours had been festive; the already friendly people of Boulder were at their best filling the café with genuine smiles and holiday cheer. The tip jar was overflowing with bills, and some of our regular customers had brought us pies to take home.

But now it was quiet. Our patrons were all off with their family or friends, and the atmosphere felt like the inside of a balloon that had let out all its air. Bruce was wearing work boots, blue jeans, and a gray hooded sweatshirt. He was more wiry than thin, and his clothes hung off him in a manner suggesting that beneath the fabric was a body taut with muscles and anguish.

I gave him space and started sweeping in the far opposite corner, but kept my eyes on him. He was hunched over a notebook feverishly jotting down notes and referring to texts. When there was no floor left to sweep but beneath his feet, I tried to break the ice by saying, "You shouldn't be working, it's a holiday."

He popped his head up, startled, and noticed for the first time that the café was closing. "Sorry," he muttered, and quickly began gathering his books to leave.

"I'm not trying to kick you out," I told him. "I'm just starting a conversation. It's a holiday, so you shouldn't be working."

"Then neither should you," he replied.

"My family's in New York, so I don't mind."

"Mine's dead, so I guess I don't mind working, either."

I decided to roll with it and asked, "What are you working on?"

He considered his answer and then replied, "The forces of nature."

And that is what hooked me. "The forces of nature...care to explain?"

He looked around the empty café. "You don't have time."

"I have all day. We're closing."

He regarded me with curiosity and then flipped the hood off his head to reveal a shaved scalp covered with soft blond fuzz.

"Got something against hair?" I asked.

"My friend in Alaska has leukemia. I'm shaving my head until his chemo is over." He rubbed his palm over his thin layer of hair. "It feels good though."

"A customer gave me a pumpkin pie this morning. I was thinking about getting some vanilla ice cream and having it for dinner. Does that sound good to you?"

He got nervous and started tapping the table with his fingers. Finally, he replied, "Yes."

Bruce waited outside while I locked up, and then we headed back to my apartment where I would have my first of many lessons about the forces of nature.

It was important that Bruce see the apartment right away, because if how I lived freaked him out, then I wanted him gone before he even had his first spoonful of pumpkin pie. Fortunately, he didn't flee. He was unfazed by the dollhouse and the twin beds, and when he entered HQ, he stopped short and stared at me like I had just told him he had won the lottery.

Bruce was most captivated by the aerial photo of town. He stood a foot's length from the wall, staring up at the image, counting the grids with one hand and tapping the side of his head with the other, his mouth moving up and down as he talked to himself while performing some kind of calculation.

"I'm looking for my sister," I told him. "The boxes X'd in black are the areas I've already searched."

"I remember her," he said, looking over his shoulder at me, making sure to establish eye contact. "I was in the airport in Seattle the day her painting on the van got ruined. I didn't recognize you, though. You look different."

"I cut my hair. Were you really in Seattle that day?"

"I had a layover on my way to Alaska. Then the rain delayed my flight. I watched the coverage for hours. I couldn't believe those people were following you."

The coincidence surprised me, and I asked, "Were you going to visit your friend with leukemia in Alaska?"

"No. I hadn't met him yet. I was going to pick morels. Know what they are?"

I shook my head, and he turned his attention back to the map but continued to talk. "Morels are very rare mushrooms that grow really well after a forest fire. They only live for a few weeks, but restaurants and food distributors pay a lot of money for them. That's where I met my friend, in the forest picking mushrooms. He didn't know he was sick yet. He'd had a bunch of tests but didn't want to miss the season."

"It's that important?" I asked.

"We both made a thousand dollars a day for three weeks straight, getting paid in cash. So, yeah, it was important to him." He placed his backpack on the floor and removed a digital camera. "Here, I'll show you what they look like."

And there he was, deep in the forests of Alaska, kneeling at the thick base of a scorched tree, pointing at a small colony of mushrooms. He left the camera in my hands and returned his focus to the aerial map, running his fingers along a northwestern section of the grid where I had not yet searched.

"I think we should start here tomorrow," he said.

I stepped closer and looked where he was pointing. "That's mostly hiking trails."

"I know. If your sister's eating a big Thanksgiving meal right now, she's probably going to want to hike it off in the morning." He circled the area we were discussing with his finger and muttered softly to himself.

I wanted to scroll through the library of images saved on his camera and glean as much information about this boy as possible, but I must have sensed even then that he was broken, and instinct instructed me not to delve too deep too quickly. I didn't want to be like Kem and run. Everyone deserves a chance, Jamie, so I shut the camera off and placed it carefully on the table next to the police scanner.

Bruce ended up spending the night in your bed. Nothing romantic passed. We didn't even kiss; there was no time for it because we were too busy talking. I told him about the past year, about Holly, the LandJet, and even about what happened in Mr. Pervy's hotel room. Bruce was a good listener; he never cut me off and asked leading questions that would send me down another narrative.

In the morning we set out to find you and drove up Wagon Wheel Road on our way to the Annie U. White trailhead. The temperature was already in the midsixties and it was not yet noon, which was warm for the end of November. Prairie dogs flocked to the road's surface to enjoy the sun-heated pavement and dodged in and out of traffic along the tall grass lining the roadside.

Bruce had been quiet from the moment we'd woken up, and I thought he

104

was embarrassed about spending the night, but once we hit the trail and began hiking, he opened up and told me his life's story. For the first nine months of Bruce's life, he had had a fraternal twin who died during the birth. Bruce's parents never told him about the stillbirth, and it wasn't until ten years later that Bruce learned about this death. He had just lost his parents in a plane crash. Both Bruce's mother and father were professional photographers and they were in Vietnam filming a documentary. They took Bruce with them everywhere they traveled, homeschooling him from exotic places like Hermsdorf, Czechoslovakia, or Siem Reap, Cambodia.

The crash occurred in Nha Trang, Vietnam. Six crew members and twenty-four of the twenty-five passengers were killed, the lone survivor being Bruce. He was then sent to live with his grandmother in Littleton, Colorado, where he attended school for the first time in his life. Things went smoothly for a while, until he was walking though the cafeteria in Columbine High School while two gunmen introduced themselves to the world. Bruce survived again, but a week later, his grandmother, who had been a picture of health, died in her sleep from a brain aneurism.

After burying his grandmother, Bruce dropped out of school and was quickly picked up by social services. They brought him to their main office in downtown Denver and explained their plans to find him a new family until he turned eighteen the following fall. Bruce acted relieved and asked for a few hours alone at his Grandma's to gather his stuff and say goodbye. He promised to return by five o'clock. By four o'clock he was on a flight to LAX where he hopped on a Quantas flight to Sydney, Australia, because no Quantas flight has ever gone down. With only a knapsack full of clothes and no ties left to anyone on the planet, Bruce decided to follow in his parents' interrupted footsteps and travel the world making documentaries.

In the fall of 2004, Bruce was living in Thailand and began working his way towards the Andaman Islands in the Bay of Bengal. By Christmastime Bruce had made it to the islands, and on December 26th he was tracking the members of the Onge tribe on a reserve on Little Andaman Island. One morning a creek suddenly ran dry in the Onge's village, and though neither the tribe members nor Bruce had any idea about the earthquake in the Indian Ocean and the tsunami it had created, the Onge knew something was amiss, and quickly spread the skulls of pigs and turtles around their small colony before fleeing to higher ground in the jungle. When the wall of water hit minutes later, all ninety-six Onge members along with Bruce survived a force of nature that claimed the lives of hundreds of thousands.

After our hike we drove back down Wagon Wheel Road. I counted at least six dead prairie dogs that had been run over by passing cars that morning. Bruce eyed the roadkill, probably wondering if a day would ever come when he would stop leaving a trail of ruin in his path.

When we got back to the apartment, Bruce stopped at the entrance of the building and said, "Now you know everything. If you don't want to spend time with me, I'll understand."

"I suppose I could say the same thing to you. I mean, after all, you just wasted two hours looking for my sister."

"That wasn't a waste of time."

"And nobody died, either."

His fingers tapped at his thighs. "You think I'm crazy, don't you?"

"Let's go mark that section off the grid," I suggested, "then figure out something to cook for dinner."

"Can we have another pie?" he asked.

"Why not?" I answered. Then added, "Life's too short," but he didn't laugh or think it was funny and I suppose it wasn't.

The Worst Lie I Ever Told

A nd so we quickly fell in love. Looking back now, I realize we were both mentally ill, but at the time I thought I had found my soul mate. Bruce worked in the Boulder Public Library restacking books and archiving magazines and newspapers. He liked restoring order and the preciseness of the Dewey decimal system. The quiet atmosphere soothed him, but mostly he chose to work there because statistically very few people ever die in a library.

Before he met me, Bruce spent all his spare time researching death, survival, and natural catastrophes. When we first spoke that Thanksgiving Day, he was reading about an iceberg named B-15A that had run into the glacier near the McMurdo Research Station in Antarctica. B-15A was blocking wind and water currents that normally helped break up the ice floes in McMurdo Sound in the summer, and now penguin colonies and several research bases were in jeopardy.

Jamie, I state this to you so factually, knowing full well you have no idea what I'm talking about. You have probably never heard of the Mc-Murdo Research Center, nor are you familiar with iceberg B-15A. Neither was I, but this was just how Bruce would talk, stating facts and figures and statistics and dates and names like B-15A, all like it was common knowledge. I suppose I knew he was strange, but it was his passion and his energy that I fell in love with.

So when we'd be walking down Pearl Street sharing an ice cream cone and he'd tell me out of the blue that twenty years ago the standard width of a coffin was twenty-four inches, but now that Americans have gotten so fat, coffins are being constructed forty-eight, even fifty-two inches wide,

I'd smile and lick my ice cream, then quickly kiss his lips so that I'd still taste sweet. Then he'd talk about his dream of moving to a small town where they had no library so he could open one up. This would make me take another lick of ice cream and kiss him again for just a little longer.

The other loveable thing about Bruce was that he put his special brand of zeal into finding you. I had begun talking to Jack and Mom every few weeks, and whenever we spoke, they would both try to convince me you were dead. They weren't being cruel, but acted like it was very important I understand you were gone. I needed a believer and Bruce never faltered. After each unfruitful search of the grid, he would return to the apartment, reference the aerial map, and flip on the police scanner listening for the next glimmer of hope, honestly believing he would pick up some clue to your whereabouts, waiting with the patience and optimism that can only be possessed by a true survivor.

Initially, sex was the furthest thing from my mind. After my fight with Mom I had closed that part of me, but a couple of months with Bruce began to change all that. I started feeling urges to touch him or sit close to him. The cravings were strong and spontaneous, but Bruce didn't feel the same way and would shut down whenever I came on to him. Then his friend in Alaska died when he caught a cold near the end of his chemotherapy. Bruce locked himself in HQ for two days. When he reemerged he said, "I'm leaving now. It's for your own good."

I tried to hug him, but he pushed me away. I shoved him back and yelled, "He had leukemia before you even met him! You had nothing to do with him dying!"

Then he said, "I love you, Liza. Too much to stay."

I was dumbfounded. These were not words I expected to hear, and my reflex was to slap him across the face and shout, "Don't you dare say that if you don't mean it!" He fell to the floor holding the cheek I had struck. I rushed to him and apologized over and over again, kissing the welt I had caused and running my hands along his scalp.

The next day when I got home from work, Bruce was waiting for me in the bedroom. He had pushed the twin beds together and stuck a constellation of glow-in-the-dark stars to the ceiling above our pillows.

One day, Bruce came rushing into the coffee shop in a state of excitement bordering on agitation. He pulled me out to the sidewalk and sat me down at one of our outdoor tables. We were surrounded by customers and some were staring after noticing the urgency in Bruce's stride. He sat across from me, handed me an article he'd found online, and said, "I think I know what happened to Jamie!"

The article was about a man who had suddenly gone missing from his family in Wisconsin after dropping off relatives at an airport in Chicago. The man left his car in the airport's short-term parking lot and hitchhiked around the nation, visiting Florida, Colorado, and Arizona, after falling into what is called a dissociative fugue, a psychiatric condition that's like amnesia and results in the individual forgetting their identity, often brought on by stress.

When I finished reading, Bruce said, "We need to get the word out to truckers! We should fax her picture and description to all the truck stops across America so they can post a flyer on their bulletin boards. I don't like the idea of her wandering the highways. It's dangerous. Truckers fall asleep at the wheel all the time or they could harm her in other ways!"

His voice was escalating and people turned their heads. "Let's not think that way," I said, clutching his hand softly.

His fingers tapped at the table beneath my grasp, and he said, "This isn't good, Liza! This is not good at all!"

I had seen this kind of behavior from Bruce before. Every few weeks an intense panic would strike, and he'd become obsessed with cataclysmic events and how we were all going to die. But I knew how to calm him. When you love a person one of the very first things you learn is how to comfort them. So I said, "Tell me about Friday the 13th again, Bruce."

He nodded and for the fifth time in as many weeks told me all about Asteroid 2004 MN4, which for a while was calculated to have a one in sixty chance of colliding with the earth on Friday, April 13th, 2029. The asteroid is three hundred and twenty meters wide and would have left a hole the size of Texas, but fortunately, after more data was gathered, astronomers determined there is actually little chance of a collision, and instead on that day, we'll be able to look into the sky and enjoy what will be the brightest and fastest shooting star we have ever seen.

When Bruce finished, he calmly said, "Thanks for that... sorry," and left the table after kissing me goodbye. The episode was over and I returned behind the counter and tried to imagine tracking an object so far away in outer space. Then I thought of you standing on the side of a highway somewhere with your thumb stuck out.

This isn't fair, but when Bruce acted crazy, it really bothered me. He had regular panic attacks and his anxieties had no base in reality. I was constantly talking him off the ledge of a nonexistent building. But he was sweet and his intentions were always good, and he was the only other person on the planet besides me who believed you were alive, so I kept him around. We searched a quadrant on the grid every day, and sometimes three or four on our days off. We never went out and had no friends, and a typical night for us involved him reading about germ warfare or any other unpreventable catastrophe and me sewing for inner peace. I had bought more leather and silver and silk and had six finished purses in the trunk of the Prius. Bruce never asked about my sewing. He didn't know about the nursery rhyme chorus, and even when he knew I'd been up all night sketching, he never asked if I was okay or if there was something wrong. And yet, when he got the hiccups, I'd spend three hours having to convince him he had indigestion and not a rare autoimmune disease.

I began to resent Bruce and all his needs and phobias. I grew jealous of the love he was taking from me and unable to return, so one day when we were hiking, I told him I was pregnant when we got to the top of the trail. It was a lie, the worst lie I ever told, and I was amazed at just how easy it was for me to be calculating and mean. This was a new dimension of my personality, and even though I didn't like what I was becoming, I couldn't stop myself from wanting to find out just how evil I could be.

Bruce took the news better than I expected. The first thing he did was kiss my belly button and put his ear to my stomach. "When did you find out?" he asked.

"Yesterday," I said. "I want to name it Jamie, whether it's a boy or a girl."

We walked down the trail slower than normal. Bruce held my hand most of the way and always stayed within arm's reach so he could catch me if I fell. When we got to the small dirt parking lot at the end of the hike, he grabbed his pack from the back seat of the Prius, removed a wad of tissues from a small interior pocket, and dropped to one knee asking, "Liza, will you marry me?"

He handed me the lump of fine paper, which was wrapped around something small and hard. My mind raced as I unraveled the bundle, and when I found the diamond ring, I should have ended the charade right then and there, but I liked feeling special and decided that for just one night it would be okay to pretend.

"It was my mother's," Bruce explained. "I carry it with me everywhere I go." He grabbed the ring from my hand and slid it onto my finger. "Perfect fit," he said, admiring the jewelry. Calmly, he rose from the ground and pulled me tightly into his arms. His actions were so slow and deliberate, for a moment I actually wanted to believe my own selfish lie.

Bruce made me ride home in the back seat "for the safety of the baby." When we got to the apartment he made me take a nap, and while I rested, he ran to the hardware store and bought every childproofing system imaginable. For dinner I suggested we celebrate and go to our favorite Mexican restaurant, but Bruce said the spicy food was bad for the baby.

That was the first night Bruce didn't go to bed at the same time as me because he was too busy researching miscarriages and stillbirths and sudden infant deaths. I stared up at the stars glowing on our bedroom ceiling and laid my hands across my belly like I was expecting to feel a small kick. The next morning Bruce was in the kitchen screwing plastic jams to the cabinet doors beneath the sink. He was wearing the clothes from our hike the day before and still had not slept.

"Ready to go look for Jamie?" I asked, trying to sound cheerful. "We only have a few quadrants left." I woke up feeling very guilty and was planning on telling him that I had gotten my period during the night and that take-home pregnancy tests aren't always reliable.

Bruce was kneeling on the floor holding a power drill. He didn't even look up. "I can't. There's too much work to do here. Go without me."

"But you always come. It's our thing."

Bruce shook his head and replied, "We got a new thing now," and began to drill.

The noise from the power tool drowned out my voice, so I unplugged it from the wall and said, "Excuse me, I wasn't done talking. Now, I'd really like it if you came and looked for Jamie with me."

"It's time to forget about her, Liza. The sooner you come to grips with that, the better it'll be for the new Jamie."

"Wait. You don't think she's alive?"

Bruce crawled across the floor and plugged the cord back into the socket. "I think I gotta get this done." He looked at me and revved the drill twice.

There were no crueler words he could have spoken, so I said, "Babe, there's plenty of time to do all that stuff. It'll be more than a year before the baby will be crawling around. Besides, we might not even be living here by then. My lease is up next month."

"You have to renew it!" he shouted. "A move would be too stressful and you could lose the baby."

"Don't talk like that."

"Look, if you still really think your sister is in Boulder, fine, go ahead and look, but you're gonna have to stop pretty soon. Understand?"

For two weeks it went on like this. Bruce didn't leave the apartment once and spent the majority of his time in HQ searching the Internet for all the possible ways our make-believe baby could die. He covered the walls of HQ with pictures of sex offenders in Colorado, New Mexico, Arizona, and Utah. "We need to learn these faces," Bruce said when he saw me staring at the photos.

"No," I said. "This room is for Jamie."

Bruce pointed at the aerial map; every grid had been searched. "She's not here, Liza. She's probably dead if you want to know the truth."

"Take that back!" I yelled at him.

He shook his head.

I wasn't looking for a shouting match, so I changed tact and in a calm voice said, "I don't feel well and there's nothing to eat. Will you run out and get me some food? I'm craving cottage cheese."

"There's too much to do," he replied, and turned back to face the computer.

I spun the back of his chair around and grabbed it by the arms. "You haven't been outside in two weeks, Bruce!" I shook the chair. "The library has called every day. You're going to lose your job. So will you please go get me some food? The fresh air will do you some good."

"Okay," he said. "In a minute."

After an hour he still hadn't left, so I walked to the store and ate the cottage cheese with a plastic spoon right at the register. By the time I got back to our building the sun was going down. I looked up to the windows of our apartment and noticed they were glowing orange. At first I thought the place was burning, but then realized the color was a reflection of the sun setting over the mountains.

Bruce had covered our windows with tinfoil and I couldn't bring myself to walk upstairs and find out why, so I got in the Prius and drove to the airport. I parked in the short-term parking lot, just like the man with dissociative fugue, and bought a ticket to LaGuardia. Staten Island was the next place to look for you. I tried hard not to think about Bruce; eventually he would be all right. He was a survivor.

Ming

Forgive me, Jamie, I fell asleep but am awake now, and it's almost five o'clock and much has happened during my afternoon of dozing. Dr. Mawji just woke me up and is sitting beside me unraveling the bandage from my hand as he gives me a lesson in the appendage's anatomy. There are twenty-nine bones, twenty-nine joints, three major nerves, and one hundred and twenty-three ligaments that make up the human hand. He tells me I'm lucky because my three major nerves were spared. In a few hours, two orthopedic surgeons, both hand specialists, will begin piecing me back together and Dr. Mawji is confident that I'll make a full recovery.

Then he asks, "How are you feeling?" and it's obvious from the tone of his voice that his concern is not for my hand but my head.

"I honestly don't know," I tell him. "It's been a really odd day and I'm actually kind of worried about a few things."

The doctor nods understandingly and asks, "Like what?"

I could tell him about Officer Ryan and the three men who posed as cops, or I could tell him that Lily and I accidentally switched purses and the disk with her secret films that everyone is after is right here beneath the sheets, but instead I tell him the truth and say, "I've been talking to my sister today."

"And that's a bad thing?" he asks unalarmed.

"I'm afraid I won't be able to stop."

Dr. Mawji dabs at the gunshot wound softly with an antiseptic cotton swab. "Know what I think?" he asks cheerfully and then stops tending my wound and gently holds my wrist. "I think you should say whatever it is you have to say and get it all out now, and then maybe take break for a while."

"Until the next time I get shot, right?" I smile so he knows I'm kidding.

He chuckles and goes back to cleaning the wound then shifts into a more doctor-like tone and tells me, "There's a waiting room full of people who want to talk to you. Two agents from the FBI's missing persons division, Chief of Police Alec Dunbar and two detectives, a private investigator hired by the Durfee family, and your mother and brother."

"Whoa." I reply, sitting up a little. "That is a lot of people."

"They all got here around two o'clock this afternoon. The police and the FBI have been insisting that I wake you, and I think I've fought them off as long as I can." He reaches for a fresh roll of gauze and then begins to wrap the bandaging around my hand, starting above my wrist, then gently around my thumb and across my palm.

It feels good to be tended so carefully, and I close my eyes and exhale a deep, tired breath. Dr. Mawji tells me he'll give me a few moments to gather myself before he sends anyone in, but right after he leaves, Officer Ryan races into the room and turns on the television. "Sleeping Beauty," he says in an obnoxious voice. "Pay attention."

He changes the channel to the local five o'clock news, which starts by showing a picture of me in my hospital bed. The volume is muted, but the right side of the screen is covered with a graphic listing all my meds. "I can't believe you really did it," I say to him.

"Ta-da!" he replies.

"You know I'll just deny it," I tell him.

"Too late."

I laugh at him. "You really know so very little. It's actually kinda cute. I've got the best PR agent in Manhattan, Amy Benton. Maybe you've heard of her? She's in the paper every week. Tall blond, has a reputation for having a foul mouth and being a man-eater, used to work for my mother. She'll make this thing vanish overnight."

"Kinda like your sister, huh?"

"So how much did they pay you for the picture?"

He checks the door before bragging, "Enough to buy me a new fishing boat."

"That's it?" I laugh. "I guess they saw you coming."

"You should have played nice. All we wanted was the films."

"I bet," I reply, still laughing at him. "I'd want 'em too if I were the mayor. I know what's on those films. The mayor's daughters making out with each other, the mayor's daughters doing drugs, the mayor's daughters having a threesome with a rap star...best of all, the mayor's daughters talking about their mom's abortion. He can pretty much kiss his political career goodbye."

Officer Ryan laughs and says, "I don't think he's too worried about it."

"He should be," I say. "Because I know where those films are and if your people don't let Lily go by six o'clock tonight I'll give them to Channel 5 for free."

Officer Ryan continues to laugh, and says, "You really are a crazy bitch, aren't you?" as he leaves the room.

Who knows if he'll take my threat seriously. I'm not going to worry about it right now, because I have my doctor's orders to follow. So let me tell you about the flight from Denver to LaGuardia. Prior to boarding the plane, I put Bruce's mother's ring in an envelope along with a note: "Got my period. Preggo test was wrong. Live on, Bruce. Love, Liza." I sent the package to my rental on Pearl Street and listed Mom's apartment as the return address, because that's where I thought I was headed.

I was ready to give up. More than a year had passed since I'd first left New York, and all I was returning home with were six purses. I felt guilty about my lie to Bruce and responsible for sending him over the edge. It was thoughtless of me not to predict his reaction, and I regretted causing so much undue trauma. I didn't like the fact that the search was now generating casualties, and I was frightened by my ability to execute such cruel intentions.

By the time the plane was somewhere between the Mississippi and Chicago, I was feeling nostalgic and even missing Bruce. I thought about all the fun times we'd had, mostly when we were searching for you, and it dawned on me that the entire Boulder area had been canvassed, and even though you hadn't been found, I was still proud of that accomplishment. It actually made me feel really good about what I'd been doing, and I looked around the plane with a feeling of satisfaction. That's when I noticed the in-flight entertainment program was being hosted by Lily Durfee. I was sitting in a middle seat in a row in the middle of the plane surrounded by dozens of little Lily Durfees in every headrest, and I had to laugh. Then I said out loud, "I'm getting closer, Jamie," and the person sitting in front of me scowled back and reclined her seat.

Then something on all the small TV screens caught my attention again. Clips of the worst contestants from the previous season's *American Idol* auditions were playing, and I began to grow nauseous as I watched and wondered whether or not we made the cut of misfits. In my seat pocket was a set of headphones wrapped in cellophane, but I chose not to listen. Halfway into the sketch we appeared, standing in front of the three judges, motionless with no rhythm and no anthem, the petrified expression on my face looking just as frozen as your mannequin's. When we scurried offstage, the camera zoomed in on the judge best known for his vitriolic sentiments, and shortly after, a wave of chuckles could be heard rolling through the aircraft.

When the plane landed it was nearly midnight, so I spent the night in the airport. I had six carry-ons, but no possessions, and hung around the baggage claim until noon the following day watching passengers collect their property and head for the exit with some place to go. I stood by a rack of brochures that offered tours of the Statue of Liberty and boat rides along the Hudson River and debated both activities until I finally went outside and saw a sky laden with charcoal-colored clouds pregnant with rain. So I hopped in a cab and asked the driver to take me to the middle of Staten Island.

The rider before me had forgotten his umbrella, which was branded with the Morgan Worth Bank logo, a notable coincidence, since Morgan Worth was where I had worked for Mr. Pervy. I understood this find to be more than chance, and kept the umbrella as my own, thus supplying me with a belonging which I hoped would somehow lead me towards a destination.

The cab driver kicked me out of the car on Port Richmond Avenue. We'd been circling several blocks in a busy section of Staten Island for some time, and he was ready to move on to a new fare. Across the street was the English Lady Fabric Store, so I entered the shop, which was empty except for the saleswomen and one other customer, an Asian man who looked to be in his midfifties. It was obvious there was something important about this man by the way the employees treated him, though he didn't speak one word and no one tried to converse with him. Workers were bringing him swatches of fabric and he would either nod or shake his head. The staff would scamper off only to return again with more samples. He had a bandage on his right hand, and I noticed him staring at my

117

purses. At one point I actually thought he was following me, but I didn't feel threatened by him. I roamed the aisles selecting some yards of leather and silk, and then bought some needles, shearing scissors, and heavy stitching cord. They sold sewing machines, but that would have been too heavy to carry around, and besides, I had bought and lost two during the search already, so it was probably best to hold off for a bit. As chance would have it, I arrived at the counter at the same time as the Asian man.

He gestured for me to check out first, smiling at his cart full of bolts of various types of fabrics as if to say his tab would take much longer to tally than mine. I thanked him and my voice echoed through the mart, catching everyone off-guard with the exception of this kind man whose only reaction was to maintain the same calm smile.

When I got outside it was raining, and I stood beneath my new umbrella with my new materials and six finished purses pondering where to go next. A few minutes later, the Asian man exited the store and stood beneath the doorway's canopy staring out at the large raindrops splattering on Port Richmond Avenue. He had no umbrella and began to cover his cartload of fabrics with his coat.

"How far are you walking?" I asked him. When he didn't respond, I added, "This is big enough for two," referring to my umbrella, "I'd be happy to share."

The man didn't look up from his cart until I approached him. When he realized I was talking to him he handed me a card that read: "Hello, my name is Ming and I am deaf and mute. If you'd like to tell me something please point at your palm."

I followed these instructions and he handed me a pen and a pad of paper on which I wrote, "May I walk you home" accompanied by a small doodle of rain bouncing off an umbrella.

When we got to his place, he wanted to thank me and invited me inside for coffee or tea. With no other place to go, I accepted.

Ming lived alone in a two-story house that was painted white with navy blue shutters and had a small, well-manicured lawn. On his front door was a sign that said RING BELL BY FLIPPING SWITCH with an arrow pointing to a light switch. Ming's only rule was that you flicker the lights any time you entered or exited a room he inhabited. This I learned on my first night, the first night of many, as I ended up staying with Ming for several weeks.

The relationship was not romantic or sexual; it was more like an apprenticeship because, as it turned out, Ming was a personal designer to the stars. He crafted blue jeans for Cameron Diaz, scarves for Lindsay Lohan, dress shirts for Howard Stern, a tuxedo for Jay-Z; the list went on and on. He had noticed my six purses the first time we crossed paths in the fabric store and was impressed with the workmanship. Over our first cup of tea he gave me a sketch of denim pants embroidered with a floral pattern on the back pockets, and he handed me a needle and thread. So I followed his design and passed what I didn't even know was a job interview. Ming had cut his right hand halving a bagel, and even though he could still sew, he was falling behind his production schedule. Working with stitches in his fingers forced him to change his technique, and as a result, his wrist was swollen. He needed help and guaranteed discretion because people were paying for his work, not mine, and I told him I understood completely.

He offered me a hundred bucks an hour along with a legally binding nondisclosure agreement. I signed the papers, but instead of taking the wages, I asked if I could sleep on his couch instead. He was hesitant to agree, but he did, and the next day I endeared myself wholly to him when I returned from Chinatown with a pair of long tweezers and a small box of yellow jackets who gave up their lives to heal his wrist with their venom.

I never really figured out why Ming allowed me to stay with him. Maybe sometimes one good deed really does deserve another, and when I offered to share my umbrella, Ming decided to repay me by sharing his home. Other than sewing, Ming had no need for me. He scheduled all his appointments via e-mail and lived within walking distance of food and groceries. His clients all traveled to Staten Island to see him, so he didn't need a chaperone or an assistant. What I did provide was company and a new wrinkle in his silent existence.

Ming enjoyed showing me his creations and at first only allowed me to help with the cutting and measuring, but eventually he handed over the needle, which always lead to him feverishly tapping his palm to interrupt with a note about how I could stitch a border differently or insert a zipper without compromising the lining. He was very patient and thoughtful with his advice, and within one month, we had gotten caught up to his production schedule, and I'd even had enough time to make four more purses, all of which ended up being bought by famous clients of Ming's, which in the end proved to be my springboard to Lily Durfee and all the success that has followed.

I will get to all that soon, there is not much time left, but let me tell you just a little more about Ming before Mom and the police and the FBI ruin our day. And in case we do get interrupted, please know that I have enjoyed our time together. I am a new person today, Jamie. The hole that was blasted through the center of my hand was the place where I've been hiding from you for the past year, and the small piece of flesh that the bullet took with it was hiding my memories and hopes and convictions and even all the uncertainties I had about you. But now that cave has been unearthed, we have been reunited, and I am grateful for that. I am grateful to have you back in my life.

But back to Ming... at night we mostly played Scrabble. He had an awesome vocabulary because he spent so much of his life reading, but it was strange to think how he'd never actually heard or spoken many of these words. Ming knew sign language, but used it as little as possible, because he worked with his fingers all day and signing tired his digits and made them bulky and more muscular, which made his work difficult.

For me, living in Ming's bubble of silence was exactly what I had needed: to remove myself from contact with all people, holing up in a plain house on Staten Island with a deaf-mute and the occasional megastar who would announce his arrival by flickering on and off the lights. I had all but given up on trying to find you. I knew that I was sick and scared the illness would follow me wherever I went next. So I lived in silence in Ming's vacuum while debating the next step.

I still had a lot of money from the sale of the LandJet and figured there was enough to live on for a couple of years while I worked on my line of purses. More of Ming's clients had inquired about the bags, and there seemed to be a true demand building.

The last week of April, Ming informed me that on the first of May he'd be traveling to London for an annual month-long visit during which he would meet with Elton John, Madonna, Gwyneth Paltrow, and others who appreciated his fashion as art. He thanked me for my company and wrote that I had changed his life in ways that he could never have predicted. Because of me, he wrote, he was going to try and find a girlfriend or wife when he returned from overseas. He made me promise that I would continue designing purses and pledged to refer his clients to me.

On my last day with Ming the lights signaling the doorbell flickered, and he handed me a note saying the visitor was a woman who wanted to talk to me about my bags. When I opened Ming's front door Lily Durfee was standing there, her hair in pigtails, wearing the Dartmouth T-shirt branded with your name.

"Liza, it's me," she said. "You look like you're staring at a ghost."

"Your shirt has my sister's name on it," I sounded like I was in a trance.

"I know. I'm sorry." Lily frowned and looked genuinely embarrassed. "I didn't even realize until I was halfway here. Do you want it? I'm sure Ming has something I could borrow."

Still in a trance, I replied, "I've been looking for her."

"I know. Everyone knows." She tilted her head and looked me in the eyes. "Do you want to talk about it?"

Lily sat me down on Ming's front steps, facing out towards the street. The Town Car that she had arrived in was double-parked, and she told the driver that we'd be a while and that he could go get lunch. Then she sat next to me and wrapped her arms around one of my knees. I felt myself beginning to cry; you have to remember that Lily was the first familiar face I had seen since I had set out for St. Petersburg. There was something very emotional about being reunited with someone who wasn't a stranger.

"I've really been struggling," I admitted. The words felt good to say out loud.

Lily put her arm around my back and said, "I wanted to talk to you about your bags, but I've also been worried about you."

So I told her about the article in *New York* magazine with her on the cover, wearing the same T-shirt she had on then, your T-shirt, Jamie, with your name on it, and how it was the catalyst to send me on a five-city search that spanned the country.

Almost an hour had passed when Ming joined us on his stoop looking confused as to why we had not come inside. But Ming could read expressions better than most and quickly discerned that our conversation was more than just business and fashion, and he sat down behind us, leaning his back against mine for support, and after a few minutes I could tell by the rhythm of his breath that he was sleeping.

I wondered if in his dreams he could speak and hear. I hoped that he could not, my theory being that waking up to a silent and unspoken world after a night of dreaming about the sound of wind blowing through trees, or waves breaking on the beach, or even the monotonous rumbling of a diesel truck, would be devastating. This reminded me of the many nights I had dreamed of you—beneath the thatched roof of Holly's bungalow in St. Petersburg, atop the LandJet in the Indian reservation in South Dakota, the night I spent in Bliss' jail, and beneath the neon stars in our bedroom in Boulder. It was why I could never sleep; because I was afraid I would dream of you and have to wake up only to realize that you were still gone.

Lily must have sensed I was thinking of you, because she stopped talking and casually rested her arm on my knee. The gesture was warm and comforting, which was exactly what I needed, because it was at that very moment I promised myself to never think about you again, to never dream about you again, because this way I would never have to experience losing you again.

And now, today, you have returned. Almost a year has passed since that April afternoon on Ming's front steps, and for the most part, I have succeeded in blocking you from my thoughts. I'm sorry if you have felt neglected. I'm sorry that I ran from you with the same suddenness with which you disappeared from me. I know how much that hurts, but I needed to get well and I can tell you today that I am better. I am now a healthy sick person, just like Ming was a fully functional disabled person. And like him, I too am now ready for a kind stranger to protect me from the rain and change my life forever. That stranger is you, Jamie, and the storm has passed, so you should know that it is safe for you to come home.

The Press Conference

———∿∿∿———

Astory is breaking on the local news. The mayor's daughters have called a press conference outside their loft in TriBeCa. The girls' hair is a mess, they're wearing ripped blue jeans and baggy long-sleeved shirts, and they're both smoking cigarettes and wearing sunglasses. Marcus is watching with me. He ran into the room a few seconds ago to warn me about the invasion that's about to take place, saying, "Looks like everyone's coming at once."

Mom's voice can be heard first, growing louder along with the fast-paced clicking of her heels against the hallway's hard floors, as she shouts, "She's my daughter and if she's well enough to talk, then I'm seeing her first!"

Marcus and I share a look, and he says, "Shall I arrest her for disturbing the peace?" We both smile and then look back at the TV.

The MDs are as inebriated and slapdash as rockers doing a press junket in the middle of a world tour. The girls can't string two thoughts together and they both keep swearing into the microphone. This is a train wreck in progress, a spectacle bizarre enough to silence even Mom, who has entered my room along with Jack, three policemen, two FBI agents, the private detective, Officer Ryan, and Dr. Mawji.

We are all staring at the TV watching the wheels peeling off the tracks and sparks flying from the tips of the MDs burning cigarettes. The MDs are wobbling in front of an arc of press, and their message is that they had nothing to do with Lily Durfee's kidnapping or the murders of Misty and Memphis.

A reporter asks, "Do you think the two crimes are connected?"

One MD replies, "We don't know anything, we just said that."

The same reporter follows up, "Are the police questioning you about your involvement in these crimes? Is that why you feel the need to make this announcement?"

The MDs look at each other and neither replies.

A different reporter shouts, "The police have made no official announcement connecting Lily Durfee's kidnapping to the shooting of the exotic dancers. Obviously you both believe the crimes are linked, can you tell us why?"

"We just do," replies the other MD.

A third reporter asks, "Are either of you concerned that making an unsolicited public denial actually makes you look guilty?"

The MD that just spoke says, "What?" then takes a drag of her cigarette.

Sirens are heard in the distance, and two police cars and a black Suburban come screeching around the corner, sending the MDs running down the sidewalk in the opposite direction. The girls make it halfway down the block before they're captured by a hulking black man wearing a suit and an earpiece. And like Lily was last night, they're thrown into the back of the Suburban and driven away per their father's orders.

The three cops, the two FBI agents, and the private eye immediately exit my room without even excusing themselves. Apparently they have a new lead. Jack has been standing at my bedside holding my good hand. When the network cuts to commercial, he leans down and hugs me.

"What the hell did we just witness?" Mom asks the room. "Liza, do you know anything about this?"

"I know all about it, Mom. I'll tell you everything in a second." I look at Officer Ryan and say, "Once this fat bunghole leaves the room."

Mom gasps, "Liza!"

"You're right, I'm sorry, that's an insult to bungholes everywhere."

Officer Ryan hasn't stopped laughing. "I'm gonna miss you, you know that?"

"Don't worry, your hands will be full once Layla turns sixteen and is pregnant in rehab with emphysema from all the Kools."

That gets under his skin, but before he can retaliate, Dr. Mawji leads him and Marcus out of the room and shuts the door. As soon as we're alone, Jack says, "And so the legend of Liza Davis grows."

Mom has her arm around him and she adds, "We may not be a normal family, but at least it's never boring, right?" She directs her gaze at me and says, "What's with you and that policeman, Liza? Are you trying to end up in jail?"

"He sold my picture to Channel 5 and told them I was on all these medications that I've never even heard of."

Jack knows I'm fronting, so to help me cover, he chimes in, "No one believes what's on Channel 5, anyway. They're all a bunch of closeted homos posing as Republicans."

Mom is laughing and shaking her head. "Hey, I used to watch that channel."

"You see," Jack says, making his point.

We're all laughing and having a good time, so I say, "I talked to Jamie today, guys," and the banter immediately halts. "Don't worry. It was good. It needed to be done. I promise, I'm not gonna disappear again." This relaxes them a little and for some reason, probably because I've been talking to you all day about the year I was gone, I say, "I'm sorry I went away like that."

Jack still hasn't let go of my hand. Mom sits on the edge of my bed and rubs my leg. "You don't have to apologize again," she says. "Everyone's past it, Liza."

"I know, and you guys are the reason I got better and I love you both very much. And I love Dad, and I love Jamie, wherever she is."

Jack and Mom nod; as is the case with so many families who have lost a member we're a much tighter group since the tragedy. I've never actually seen a cloud with a silver lining or a pot at the end of a rainbow, but in my short, densely packed life, I have learned how to make some pretty decent lemonade. We have a family recipe now, and the ironic thing is, the main ingredient is that you're still missing.

Saturn's Return

Visiting hours are over and Jack and Mom just left. We're gonna have to call it quits pretty soon too, because my surgery is coming, but there's still a lot to tell and it's getting late, so let's go back to the day I left Staten Island. By the time Lily and I finished talking, I'd decided to return home. I hugged Ming goodbye right there on his doorstep, and we both got teary and even Lily was a little misty eyed. It really wasn't that sad though, because I knew I'd see Ming again, and I have many times. He continues to mentor me with my designing and has kept his promise of accessorizing the stars with my creations. Ming was and is a huge reason for my success, as is Lily's show, *Silly Little Rich Girl*.

When Lily first told me about the show, I was apprehensive. We were riding in the back of the Town Car that had driven her to Ming's, smack-dab on the middle of the Verrazano Bridge, when she launched into her pitch for me to be her sidekick.

"Me?" I said. "What do you want me for?"

"People know you, Liza. I don't think you realize just how famous you are."

"Come on." I laughed and looked over the water beneath the bridge.

Lily gazed out her window and replied, "You've got something known as dynamic fame. You're a pop curiosity, a microcelebrity."

She was snowing me and it pissed me off. So in a bitchy tone, I said, "I can't believe you're wearing Jamie's T-shirt."

Lily kept looking out the side of the car. "I'm sorry, I really didn't do it on purpose."

I continued to look out my window as well. "Everything you do is on purpose, Lily. You're whole life is on purpose."

126

She faced me and said, "Damn, girl. I liked Jamie, that's why I saved the shirt. I thought you'd be touched."

I tugged her sleeve and said, "If you hadn't worn this on the cover of *New York* magazine, my life would probably be a lot different right now."

"What would it look like?"

I shrugged. "I don't know. I'd probably still be working at Morgan Worth Bank and possibly fucking my boss."

Lily furrowed her brow. "Is that what you want?" This was a rhetorical question because she knew me better.

We were off the bridge and I missed being over the water. "Obviously not, but I didn't look for Jamie because I wanted to be famous, either. I wanted to find her."

Lily grabbed my hands. "Listen, if you do the show, you could get the word out to a lot of people about Jamie, but the thing is, Liza, I think you need to stop looking for her." She squeezed my hands to make sure she had my attention, and added, "You've done everything you can, and it's been touching and heartbreaking and inspiring, but it's not healthy."

The car was whizzing along, and all of a sudden we were surrounded by blackness, traveling underwater through the Battery Tunnel from which we emerged into Manhattan, the last place on the roster to look for you. Not only had I come full circle, but I was riding in the back seat of a Town Car with Lily Durfee, the girl whose picture had inspired my search, and she was telling me it was time to stop. The city had not changed. It was still dirty and beautiful and bustling and lonely and filled with millions of unique faces. I started to cry again, and Lily grabbed my hand and said, "You've got a year's worth in there so let 'em all out."

So I laughed as I cried and nodded my head as we crawled uptown through rush-hour traffic. After a few minutes, I said, "I guess I'm gonna need a job," which was basically an admission I was quitting my search. "How much do these TV gigs pay?"

We were stopped at a light and Lily was staring through the windshield at a pedestrian in the crosswalk wearing a T-shirt with Andy Warhol's portrait of Marilyn Monroe on the front. "Well, I can't say exactly, you'll have to sign with my agent first, but I'm sure you'll get at least six figures and the shoot won't last longer than fifty days."

"Sounds like good work if you can get it," I said.

Lily nodded. "If we do this right, we'll make a lot more, but I'll explain all that tomorrow. Why don't you sleep on it, okay?"

I agreed, and we crept uptown in our insulated silence surrounded by delivery trucks and busses and cabs. While stopped at another intersection, a black woman on the sidewalk caught my attention. Her hair was tangled and dyed orange from peroxide, and she was heavyset and walking the weary stride of a soul exposed to a lifetime of hardships. She was wearing tattered jeans and a very large hockey jersey with the name of a famous player printed in big, bright letters across her shoulders. The player's captain "C" adorned her left chest, and it was clear the woman hadn't bought the shirt and almost certainly had no idea whose name was branded on her back. This woman was one bad decision away from being homeless and two away from death. Lily was watching her too, and she said, "You know what the problem with life is? Sometimes it's just too damn relentless for people to even catch their breath."

When the car pulled up in front of Mom's apartment building, Lily wrote down the name and number of her psychiatrist and handed it to me, saying, "We all need a little help now and then."

I looked towards the lobby. Mike, the doorman, was approaching to open up the back door for me. "I haven't seen my mom in a year," I said. "I don't even know if she'll let me upstairs."

Lily grinned and replied, "Of course she will."

Mike opened the door, and I turned to Lily, and all I could think to say was, "Thanks for the ride." She probably thought I was referring to our commute from Staten Island, but I was actually talking about the entire past year.

Mike let me right into the building and sent me up the elevator without calling to announce my arrival. This was nice and made me feel at home. I've often wondered if Mike had made me wait to ring upstairs, if I would have gotten cold feet and ran. As I rode up the elevator, I grew more and more worried about seeing Mom again, wondering what she'd be most upset at me for: running away, stripping for her lover, or getting her fired from the most important job she'd ever had?

When the elevator doors opened into the foyer, I could see her reflection in the den's window that faces Central Park. She was standing off to the right wearing a terrycloth robe, and her hair had just been blown dry. She was using scissors to cut a tag off a new Hermès scarf, and her head was raised from hearing the sound of the elevator. I froze at the edge of the hallway, wishing I could hide or make myself invisible. But there was no cover, so I stepped into her sight and said, "I didn't find her."

Mom dropped the scarf and froze with the blades of the scissors open. She literally didn't move for at least five seconds and just stared at me in amazement. She looked younger. Her hair was growing out, the bags under her eyes were gone, and she'd gained just enough weight to look healthy again. She actually looked a lot like you. Her silence freaked me out, but then she said my name as she put down the scissors and ran over to wrap her arms around me. I don't know how long she held me for, several minutes at least, and when we finally separated, both of our shoulders were wet from each other's tears.

When we'd caught our breath, I said, "We should have called the police the first day she was gone." I stepped out of the hug so we could see each other's faces. "How could we just let her go like that?"

"Don't, Liza. None of us thought she was in danger. You know how Jamie was, it's not like that was the first time she disappeared."

"Well, it was the first time she didn't come back and you just pretended like everything was *business as usual*."

Mom pulled the lapels of her robe together with one hand and grabbed my fingers with the other. "I looked for her, Liza, and I looked hard. I hired the best people and called in every favor I had, and when that didn't work, I went all the way to Tulsa to see a psychic; that's how desperate I was."

I was still holding on to Mom's hand and didn't want to let go. Her grip was tight, but not in a bad way. "You were keeping it a secret, though, even the stuff about the psychic and the detective. Why would you do that?" I was unsure where all these questions were coming from, but asking them felt like the right thing to do.

Mom was prepared to answer, like she'd been waiting a long time for the opportunity. "Because I thought that was my job, and not as CEO, but as your mother. You and Jack still had hope, and I didn't want to take that away from you. I figured what could be the harm, right?"

"I think I pretty much answered that question," I said.

Mom pulled me into a hug again and spoke softly into my ear, "Hey, you're home now. We'll get you some help ASAP." The she grinned and said, "Not Dr. Graves, though."

"Can I have something to eat?" I wasn't hungry but wanted to be fed, by Mom, so we went into the kitchen and sat at the same old breakfast table where you, me, and Jack would goof around before school. Mom brought me a plate of chicken salad and orzo she'd bought at the deli on 92nd and Madison and sat with me. "You look pretty," I said. "Are you going out?"

Mom waved her hand and said, "Oh, I had a charity thing at the MOMA, but I'm not gonna go now."

"You can go," I said.

"I don't want to go."

"What do you think happened to her?"

"I don't know, sweetheart."

"I don't even remember what the last thing I said to her was. It was probably something stupid like, 'good night' or something." I took a bite of the pasta and it tasted good.

Mom watched me eat for a few minutes, then said, "I'm sorry I didn't look for her sooner. The night she ran away, we got in a big fight at three in the morning. I had said good night to her dressed in a bathrobe and slippers like I was going to bed, but then I snuck out to see Tim once I thought everyone was asleep."

I was about to take a bite and was so surprised the food fell off the fork. "Mr. Purdy? You were seeing him all the way back then?"

"Longer than that, I'm afraid." Mom grabbed the fork, scooped up the food I'd dropped, and ate it. "Anyway, when I came home that night Jamie was standing outside smoking a cigarette. You know how I feel about smoking, so you can imagine my reaction, but Jamie was even more indignant. She wasn't naïve and quickly put the pieces together, and we had it out right there underneath the building's awning. Mike was the doorman on duty that night, and he was so embarrassed, he closed the door and took the elevator to the basement. I buzzed him about five minutes later as Jamie stormed off down the block. That was the last time I saw her. So when we didn't hear from her, I really just thought she was letting me have it."

Mom passed me the fork and I pushed some orzo into a neat pile and left it there. "But you didn't really look for me either."

"I knew you were going to leave before you even left, Liza. It's all you talked about for six months. I did try and find you, though. After our fight. When you were in Florida, your voice sounded so different, it had dropped three octaves, and I was really worried."

130

"You disconnected your phone, Mom."

"Not because of you, because of Tim. I broke it off with him after our fight and he went berserk. I was really very worried about you, so I sent the same detective I hired to find Jamie down to Florida to find you. We knew you were somewhere near Tampa, but every lead was a dead end, and the detective said it was like trying to find someone in the witness relocation program."

"Why didn't you just call me? I didn't disconnect my phone."

"Because I thought we should speak in person."

"In person via a private eye?" I looked at her skeptically. "Sorry, but I don't get it."

Mom dropped her head a little and said, "He was going to bring you home."

I sat back and folded my arms. "What if I didn't want to go home?"

"Then he would have used force."

"Jesus, Mom."

"Well, if you didn't want to come home, don't get mad at me for not trying to bring you home, which I did, anyway." We both laughed at the same time because we were fighting again, in circles, just like a mother and daughter. Mom continued, "When Jamie went missing it was like, poof, she was gone. But you, you started showing up everywhere. First on the Home Shopping Network, then on CNN. It broke my heart when I saw you sitting in the back of that van with the mannequin." She got a distant look in her eyes and said, "I was in the Red Carpet Club in Amsterdam waiting to fly home from a meeting, and I looked at the TV, and there you were, driving down the highway in Oregon being followed by hundreds of people." She shook her head and laughed. "So I hopped on the next flight to Seattle, and by the time I had landed you'd been arrested in Bliss, so I flew to Idaho to bail you out, but you were already gone."

"You flew to Idaho?" I asked in disbelief.

Mom nodded, her smile growing even larger. "By the way, the man who bought the LandJet was looking for you a few months ago. I guess a blizzard hit Utah this winter and the rest of the paint dripped completely off the van. I think he wanted his money back."

We laughed some more and I said, "I'm sorry I got you fired."

"Don't be. I should have quit long before then. If anyone's sorry, it's me."

"Are you?" I felt badly for grilling her, but realized I was asking Mom all these questions for you, Jamie. I was confronting her for the both of us, so that when I forgave her, you'd be forgiving her too, because it was time for the three of us to move on.

"I am," Mom said. "Really." She looked me in the eyes and I nodded to let her know I believed her. "The detective picked your trail up again in Boulder when you opened up a bank account, but by that point it was obvious you were in the middle of something very cathartic, so rather than interrupt, Jack and I decided together to let you live it out."

I couldn't believe my ears. "But every time we talked you guys told me to come home."

"Well, don't be mad, but I did hire a grad student to check on you, and he'd e-mail me from your coffee shop every morning to let me know you were okay."

"You had me followed?" The hair on the back of my neck stood up.

"No, not followed. All he did was let me know you'd shown up at work every day so that we knew you were alive. But we did come and visit once." I wished you could have seen the look on Mom's face, Jamie. She was absolutely tickled. "It was fun. We hired a make-up artist in Denver to put prosthetics on our faces. She made Jack look a hundred pounds heavier and gave me a big nose and high cheekbones."

I looked down at my plate and realized the food was almost gone. "I don't believe you," I said.

Mom's smile was authentic. "The day we were there, a boy came running into the coffee shop and dragged you right out to the table next to ours. We thought for sure you'd spot us, but this boy was in a panic because he thought Jamie had amnesia or something. We watched you calm him down, and I remember when you guys left, Jack said to me, 'Mom, why are you crying?' and I said, 'Because I'm proud of your sister, honey.'"

Mom slid the plate over to her side of the table and was about to stand up with it, when she said, "That boy showed up here a few weeks ago. He said he was the father of your child."

"I'm not pregnant," I told her. "I never was."

"I see," she stood up and grabbed the dirty plate from the table.

"I really didn't know about you and Mr. Purdy, Mom. I swear."

"It's okay, honey. Everything needed to happen exactly the way it did. It was all part of my Saturn return."

You heard right, Jamie. In her retirement, Mom has found astrology. She explained that every thirty years, Saturn returns to our chart and forces us to line up our ducks and pay karma's piper. It didn't matter that Mom's Saturn was ten years early, she fully believed losing her job and her lover had been written in the stars. We all seek peace differently; I sew, Mom looks to the heavens, and whatever you did, Jamie, I hope that you found it.

Mom pulled me out of my seat to give me a hug. She was still in her robe and looked very comfortable and casual. "You seem really good, Mom," I said. "You seem happy."

"I am happy," she replied. "I'm happy you're home."

So I forgave her, Jamie; for you, for me, and even for Saturn who returned to Mom early, quite possibly because you never did.

The Hit List

I called Lily's psychiatrist the next day and she knew who I was. She remembered the interview I did with your mannequin in the back of the LandJet in Pocahontas and had seen footage of me at the gas station in Echo, Oregon, lying down on the pavement in my bathing suit while muttering to myself. She was eager to talk to me, and cleared her entire afternoon of appointments, so that we could meet for a large block of time. Apparently she thought I could use the extra sessions, and she was right.

The day after that, I met with Lily's agent and an executive from the network and signed on for ten episodes of *Silly Little Rich Girl*. Lily invited me to her apartment after the meeting, and she knew even then the show would be a hit because she told me she wanted to invest in my *LD* bag company.

"I've made less than twenty bags, Lily, it's hardly a company," I told her.

"It will be," she said.

We had three months until filming, and my job for those ninety days was to design and produce a line of eight different purses. Ming helped me find a local manufacturer, and we made five hundred of each style and launched a website to sell them. The night before the online store went live, Lily wore a short skirt and white cotton underwear on which she wrote "ldbags.com," and when the paparazzi photographed her climbing out of a limo later that night, the resulting picture made the rounds the next morning. By the end of the day, we had sold over thirty percent of our inventory with orders from as far away as Australia, Japan, and South Africa. I was astounded, but Lily didn't seem that shocked. All she had to say was, "I've had so many scumbags aim a lens up my skirt, I can't believe I didn't think of this sooner." The next night she went out and wrote "Obama!" down there and that got even more attention. As a joke we started selling "Paparazzi Proof Panties" on ldbags.com branded with "Brazilian!" or "Space for Rent." People ordered those too, and didn't care that every style was "out of stock" (because there was no stock to begin with), and didn't mind waiting four to six weeks for the underwear's arrival.

I learned a lot about Lily during those three months. Everyone at Dartmouth knew how smart she was, but even there we'd underestimated her. At first I thought the only reason she was doing the show was for money and maybe for the challenge of tricking viewers into thinking her thirty-minute infomercial was reality TV, but then Lily came up with the ploy of having her guests sign waivers and hanging a notice on her door, because she figured most people wouldn't read the fine print and assume the paperwork was for her show and not a personal project. Her guests would be drunk and on their way to a party, and at two in the morning no one is thinking clearly, anyway. She quickly became obsessed with the possibilities and chose specific targets. Her hit list included a pop star who couldn't sing, a stage mom so hungry for fame she compromised her daughter to keep her in the headlines, an actress who pretended to be a vegetarian and was a spokesperson for PETA even though she loved to eat meat, any scientologist, a God-fearing Jesus-loving talk-show host who had a not-so-secret hatred of Jewish people, and a sixteen-year-old girl who was a notorious slut but had made millions and millions of dollars selling herself as a virginal tween. The MDs weren't even in Lily's sights, but things sometimes have a funny way of working out.

Lily told me about her hit list the day she was installing all the hidden cameras in her apartment. She was on a ladder in her living room, doing the wiring herself, as she explained, "*Silly Little Rich Girl* isn't going to be true reality TV. Nothing branded 'reality TV' is real. Sure, they can put a few cameras in a washed-up celebrity's home and we can see how dysfunctional his family is, but it's still contrived because they know they're being filmed. There's only one way to find out who a person truly is, and that's to get them drunk and make them feel safe."

I was lying on her couch, nauseous from new meds my psycho pharmacologist wanted me to try, and watching Lily teetering on top of the ladder

135

wasn't helping. "So how'd you come up with the list? I mean, what did those people do to you?"

"Me, personally? Nothing. They're just easy targets." I gave Lily a bewildered and slightly disapproving look, and then closed my eyes and rested my head on a pillow. She continued, "I don't want to be remembered as a ditzy model, Liza. I want to be remembered as the ditzy model who showed the world what true reality television really is."

I didn't lift my head or open my eyes, just said, "Who says anyone's gonna remember you in the first place?"

Lily laughed. Her reply was, "Well, they will now."

Lily threw a party every night of the forty-six days of production. Misty and Memphis were her hired guns. She had found them a month before filming began, made them sign NDAs, and paid them a lot of money to grease the social wheels and use their beauty and seductiveness to cloud everyone's judgment. No one knew they were strippers; some nights they posed as actresses, or models, or heiresses. I didn't go to most of those parties. I was working on my sleeping patterns and trying to get my biorhythms in check. I was living in Mom's apartment, and she made a point of being home every night except for one week when she went to Taos for a breath work seminar.

Lily managed to nail half her targets. The night the PETA actress was in town, Lily had Nobu cater her party, and the phony vegan couldn't resist their famous Kobe beef. The stage mother was a frequent visitor to the apartment, and one night Lily filmed her trying to buy drugs for her daughter who had just gotten out of rehab. Another night the hidden camera caught her saying, "Well, she's done the sex-tape thing, she's been photographed not wearing any underwear, she's had a DUI, and she's been to rehab, so we're not sure what's next. Probably either a pregnancy or a lesbian relationship. We're meeting with people about both options right now." The tycoon tween had good handlers who kept her from coming to Lily's parties, and the talk-show host with the anti-Semitic views got pregnant and was off the social circuit. As for scientologists, they were the only people who refused to sign the waivers to be let upstairs. That left only the lip-synching singer, whom Lily managed to expose legitimately on our show.

The singer was a Canadian goody-goody white-teethed happy person who was much more of a marketing sensation than a songstress. She was rumored to have a hideous voice and lip-synch her concerts, which she denied vehemently in all her interviews. She was signed to a major label, had a great PR team, and her videos were sexy but not suggestive; she perfectly embodied the definition of America's Sweetheart, the one snag being she was from Canada. While we were filming, the girl's latest CD came out, and she did a big signing at a store in Times Square, so we decided to crash the party with a karaoke machine.

Teenage girls were wrapped around the block dressed up like the pop star, and they went wild when we showed up. Everyone was taking turns performing the singer's hits while waiting in line for her autograph. The reps from the label loved the surprise until the crowd passed the mic over to the pop star, who, after much cajoling from the unruly pack, agreed to do one of her songs. Needless to say, her recital was as harmonious as an alley cat being tortured, and we captured every brutal missed note for the show.

Lily turned to me halfway through the singer's performance and whispered into my ear, "Like candy from a baby," and it was at that moment that I understood the cosmic connection between Lily Durfee and my search for you. When I had seen her on the cover of *New York* wearing your jeans and the shirt with your name, I started to believe she would have the answer to where you were, but in that record store, I realized instead she had the answer to who you were. And you were nothing like her, Jamie. I love Lily, but she is jaded, and that can rarely be fixed. Life is full of events that harden our skin and insulate our souls; unwatched hearts will turn cold and minds will close. The condition can turn into a walking form of death, and sadly, Lily has already taken her first steps. But your legacy is intact, Jamie. You will forever be the peace-loving idealist who wanted to feed babies, not steal their candy, and that knowledge alone was enough to make every single misguided decision I made over the past two years worthwhile.

That was my favorite day of filming, but not because we exposed another idol. What brought me so much joy were all the girls waiting in line in their costumes, speaking their banter and laughing their giddy, nervous laughter as they sang their pop anthem to each others' cheers. I wanted to pull each and every one of them aside and tell them that innocence is a luxury, but that is a job for a being greater than me, and in due time, each and every one of those girls will learn it on her own.

Where the Heart Is

—〰—

It's been a long day, Jamie. In about half an hour, I'm going to be moved to pre-op, where they will take some blood and run some tests before they begin to repair my hand. The doctor told me I shouldn't be nervous, and I'm not, but I'll probably be pretty out of it for a while, so I guess I should say goodbye. Time is passing; don't wait too long before you decide to come home. Jack is quickly turning into a man and the years are smoothing Mom's rough edges. We miss you every day, but we are also moving forward, because we know that is what you would want us to do.

In case you're wondering, I've either heard from or kept in touch with a lot of the people I met on my road trip. Holly sent my Certified Yodeler's certificate to Mom's apartment along with a jar of honey and ten crisp one hundred dollar bills. I don't know what the money was for, it doesn't really mean that much to her and she knows it doesn't mean that much to me, so I think it was some kind of joke. I don't really hear the chorus any more, but when I get anxious, I still sew and always make those same canvas totes I started down at her place. I send her the finished product and watch her show on the HSN to see your three twins holding the bags. Holly says they always sell out, but she never has more than ten or twenty of them in stock. They're only $29.95 and no one knows they're LD bags, if they did, they'd probably pay ten times that much. We're not in it for the money; we're in it for the memories, which are priceless, anyway. I'm thinking about asking Mom and Jack to go down to Holly's place this Christmas. I haven't asked Holly yet. If she's up to her old tricks she may not want too many visitors, but who knows, maybe she'll need me to row another crate of honey out to her friend's boat, and if she asks, I'll probably do it. That's what life is for, right?

Speaking of life, Bruce and I are friends again. He was pretty pissed at me, and rightly so, but once I got my head on straight, I tracked him down and we had a good long talk. It probably sounded funny coming from me, but I told him he needed psychiatric help and he actually listened. He's living in Leadville, Colorado, which is a very small mining town at an elevation of almost 11,000 feet, and I suspect he chose the location because the high mountains are the safest place to live in the event of a nuclear attack, a bird flu epidemic, a West Nile outbreak, global warming floods, or just about any other kind of catastrophe. He is better though. He works in their small library five days a week and volunteers in the town's clinic Sundays because he's "tired of being a curse." He sends me an e-mail every few months. His letters never have much of a point except to let me know he's still alive.

Mr. Pervy is still living too, but right now probably in a place that quite resembles hell. He was arrested for luring a minor over the Internet, and even though he's a rich, white, powerful man and will probably beat the rap, they're holding him in Riker's Correctional Facility just across the Hudson River east of Manhattan. You can see the jail from the Triboro Bridge, and whenever I'm crossing that body of water, I look towards the bleak brick building and wonder which barred window he's stuck behind. I'm sure the boys love him; from what I understand pedophiles are very popular in the clink. And if he's somebody's bitch, let's just hope they're not kissing him on the mouth.

Ming did exactly what he said he'd do and met and fell in love with one of Britain's most talented and respected old-school actresses. He's moving over there to live with her in London, and I told him if he comes back signing with an English accent, I'd kill him. Actually, I'd never do that; Ming commissions me at least once or twice a month to do a handmade bag for his famous clients. They pay a silly amount of money, and unlike the bags on the HSN, everyone knows it's my brand those mannequins are carrying. There's no better advertising except for maybe a thirty-minute infomercial disguised as a reality show.

Some of the people who met you on our trip have kept in touch as well. The *American Idol* producers asked us to audition again the next season, and someone from the Party in Pocahontas offered to make you the Master of Ceremony for the next PIP, but I had to turn them both down. I told them the mannequin was stolen and burned in Seattle, which they already knew, but both seemed to think I could get another one of you. If only it was that easy.

Sorry, but Marcus is knocking. He's the only one left on guard. Officer Ryan split right after the MDs' press conference. Hopefully we'll never hear from any of them again. Marcus cracks the door open, peeks his head in the room, and then softly says, "Miss Davis, I think there's someone coming to see you. You want me to turn them away?" He looks down the hallway at the approaching visitor.

I sit up and push my hair to the side of my face and ask, "Do you like me, Marcus?"

The question catches him off-guard, and he steps into the room and closes the door behind him. "Of course I like you, Miss Davis."

"Do you think I'm dumb?"

"Not at all."

"How about crazy?"

He smiles and says, "You're definitely different, but it's a good different."

I'd been avoiding his eyes since he walked in the room, but now I look at him and ask, "Will you have dinner with me tomorrow night?"

My question hangs in the air for a moment, and then he asks, "You mean like a date?" His expression is blank until a slight twitch at the corner of his lips grows into an all-out smile.

I smirk at him and I reply, "Yeah, just like a date, but you got to promise that you'll call me Liza."

"I can do that, Liza," he says and opens the door to the hallway, and in walks Lily Durfee. Marcus winks and leaves Lily and me alone as she rushes to my bed and drapes me in a hug.

If today were yesterday, we would probably erupt into hysterical screams of joy, but there is something different about us now. We are neither hardened nor defeated, but we are wiser and more composed. Lily runs her hands along my scalp and says, "I'm so sorry. This was not meant to happen."

I smile to let her know I'm fine and ask, "It wasn't a stunt though, right, Lily?"

Lily shakes her head. "No, no, no, honey, this was very real." She reaches for my hand and kisses it.

Her tender gesture makes me sigh, and I close my eyes and exhale. Lily is still holding my hand, and she strokes my arm and leans over to kiss my forehead. "Thanks," I say and we let go of each other and sit in silence. The hospital feels as if it has been emptied of all its patients and doctors and nurses and gurneys and machines. Our room is perfectly still, and we sit steeped in a true calmness that I have only experienced once before, this morning with Marcus.

Then I tell her, "The MDs just had a total meltdown."

"I know. That's when they let me go." She raises her eyebrows suspiciously.

I reach beneath my sheets and hand over her disk. The plastic case is warm from my body and my skin has left a sweaty thigh print. Lily hops out of her seat, slides my LD bag off her shoulder, and exchanges it with her bag on the windowsill, quickly slipping the disk into the side compartment and zipping it shut. "By the way," she says, "that's an impressive assortment of pills you travel with."

"I'll explain it to you later," I tell her.

She looks at me from the corner of her eye and breezily replies, "No need, Liza."

"So what are you going to do with the disk?" I ask her.

She grins and replies, "Well, I can't just keep it all for myself."

"Lily!" I say, not in the least bit surprised. "They *kidnapped* you, for Christ's sake."

She shrugs. "It's a hot property."

"Burn it." I tell her.

"Hey," she replies, "not everyone has the Virgin Mary appear on the side of their car, okay? Now it's my turn to cash in."

I roll my eyes and shake my head, but it is all in jest, because I expect nothing less of Lily than to come out fighting and finish what she started. I had my search for you and Lily's films are her search for herself. Hopefully, she'll find what she's looking for.

Lily sits down by my bed and says, "I have a plan. How would you like to take a trip around the world with me? We can film our travels and sell it once we get back as a spin-off. We'll call it, *Silly Little Globe Trotters*."

I smile and say, "Actually, I've been thinking about getting an MBA. You could join me and we'll call the show *Silly Little School Girls*. The network will pay our tuition."

Lily smiles back and suggests, "Or we could get married and do a show called *Silly Little Bridesmaids*."

I nod and say, "And when we have kids, we can do *Silly Little Soccer Moms.*"

Lily gasps, "I'll never be a *soccer mom!*" Then she laughs and says, "Seriously. I'm going to travel and I want you to come with me."

The offer is tempting. I could start a new search across the globe and maybe this is where I'd find you—trading spices in Zanzibar, living in a tree house in Costa Rica, or watching a cricket match in Bombay. The possibilities are endless, but I have to say no.

Every Sunday night Mom, Jack, and I have dinner at her apartment. Mom doesn't cook, but she orders the fare, and though she'd never admit it, after every meal there is always enough food left over for a fourth person. Maybe this is where I will find you Jamie: at home, where the heart is.